THE FREEMASON
CIPHER

THE FREEMASON
CIPHER

QUINN MUCCIO

Charleston, SC
www.PalmettoPublishing.com

The Freemason Cipher

Copyright © 2021 by Quinn Muccio

First Edition

Paperback ISBN: 978-1-68515-425-7
eBook ISBN: 978-1-68515-426-4

Dedicated to
Poppy and Nanny,
Mark W. Malcolm,
Dan Hanson,
and
many others

TABLE OF CONTENTS

PROLOGUE

Bryan, a twenty-two-year-old college student, is studying religion and US history. He lives in Washington, DC, and is finishing up his thesis for his master's degree in religious studies. He has spent many summers in Tuscany at his family's villa and there learned all about Roman and Italian history. He went to mass with his Catholic parents; that's what got him interested in religious studies and the history behind religion. His father is a banker and his mother a historian; this has led to an eye for detail and a good mental grasp on money—the family is very well-off.

Bryan drove to the lecture hall at Georgetown University, confident and ready to deliver his thesis on religion to his classmates. He was unaware of and unprepared for the tantalizing chain of events that would follow that very day, turning his whole world upside down and changing what he thought he knew forever.

CHAPTER 1

THE CIPHER

B ryan stood there with fear on his face, with tired eyes staring right back at him amid the vast group of his peers who were listening to his lecture. "In the present-day United States, Freemasons are a group bound by history and legend, but the truth lies within the dark corridors of their humble abode," said Bryan.

"The first thing you should know about the Freemasons is that they are a secret society," Bryan said as he paced back and forth across the wooden stage. The stage creaked with each one of his steps. "A society so secretive that it was potentially the core building block of American society." The dean of the school, Dr. Andrews, a short, portly middle-aged man, walked into the room and stood in the back listening.

"Now, Freemasonry was properly founded in 1717 by our forefathers, and later came names like Benjamin Franklin and our first president, George Washington." Dean Andrews walked up from the back of the room and cut Bryan off by pointing at this watch and grabbing the microphone from his hand.

"Now we will resume this discussion tomorrow at ten a.m. Please be prompt," said Dean Andrews. All the restless students practically leaped out of their chairs and ran for the door. Dean Andrews walked over to Bryan. "Bryan, why do you study such strange subjects? Shouldn't you be studying real history instead of indulging yourself in myths and legends?"

"Well, Dean, I happen to believe that you can't mistake historical facts, and quite frankly, sir, I believe that a myth or legend is quite a fact of its own," said Bryan. Bryan smiled and tapped Dean Andrews on the shoulder as he left the auditorium and walked several blocks from the confines of the college campus.

Bryan got in his car, a black Ford Escape, and shut the door. His heart stopped as he saw a man's face in his rearview mirror. The man in the back seat of the car took out an ostensibly fully armed black pistol and shouted, "Take me to the National Archives Museum now! Just look at the road, not back at me!"

Bryan began to panic, and the sweat started pouring down his face as he stammered. "Yes, sir." Bryan drove the man up and down the streets until they finally arrived at the front of the National Archives Museum.

Bryan was drenched in sweat now and worrying about when this whole thing would be over. "Don't follow me," the man demanded as he got out of Bryan's car and walked up the steps. Bryan thought for a long moment, took a deep breath, and decided to get out of the car. He walked to the front of the museum, then skipped every other step as he ran up the stone stairs.

His legs were shaking, and his heart was beating like a fast-paced drum.

Bryan slowed his pace so as not to attract any attention as he opened the front door and walked into the building, a building that was filled with secret documents. He noticed heavily armed guards at each entry and exit point. Bryan looked desperately for the man he had seen in his car minutes prior. The man he was following had vanished into thin air, like a vapor of smoke escaping through a vent. Bryan walked steadily across the shiny marble floor, still looking for the man who had pulled a gun on him just moments before.

Trying not to attract attention, he walked around the crowded building, admiring each document as he went by. Each document was encased in thick bulletproof glass and was carefully guarded by infrared lasers and motion sensors. Not catching sight of the man, Bryan walked out of the building the way he had come in and got back into his car, discouraged yet relieved because he didn't know what he would have done if he had caught up with the gun-handling swindler. Bryan sat there, puzzled. "Why here?" Bryan questioned as he held his fist under his chin.

Bryan looked into the back seat of his Ford Escape and realized that the man had left a small yellow file behind in his extreme urgency to get out of the black sedan. Bryan grabbed the file and opened it; he saw a copy of the Declaration of Independence. There were notes in the margins detailing something that he couldn't quite make out because of the man's poor handwriting. What possibly could these words be? What could they mean?

Bryan drove to the Library of Congress in search of something there that might help him figure out what the man with the black pistol was after. As Bryan sped down the road, there were millions of thoughts swirling through his head: "Who was that man?"; "What did he want with me?"; "Or is he after the document, the scribbled-over copy of America's greatest, most sacred piece of history, written by our forefathers, who founded the building blocks of this great nation we call America?"

These questions rolled over and over in Bryan's mind, pounding in his head like raging ocean waves against a rocky shore. Bryan thought if he suddenly dismissed them, they would go away like the group of college students he had lectured to less than an hour before. Unlike the students, the thoughts and questions just kept arising in his mind. Moments later Bryan jerked his mind back to his present, dangerous reality and away from the endless questions and raging thoughts filling the crevices of his mind. He parked a few blocks away from the Library of Congress.

He took a deep breath and, with his hand shaking, grasped the door handle, hesitantly looked to the left and to the right, opened the door of his black sedan, and cautiously stepped out into the street, shutting the sedan door. He looked toward the massive building and forced himself to put one foot in front of the other. Bryan gripped the file with such intensity that it seemed as if his life was dependent upon it.

Bryan willed his nimble, thin body to walk up the cold stone steps of the library as quickly as he could without slipping or falling until he got to one of the many doors that led into the vast chamber of old paper and cowhide. Bryan felt the cool metal handle of the transparent glass door, pulled the door wide open, and slipped in.

In front of him, he saw a group of brown circular tables perfectly interlaced. Beside each small table sat a small chair with a high back, and mounted above the table was a lamp where each novelist or researcher could immerse themselves in the joys of a spellbinding anthology of history.

With the file safely gripped in his hand, he carefully placed it on one of the small, curved desks that was away from most of the visitors. He sat down and opened the file as dozens of words dauntingly stared back at him, small scattered words blotched with black ink. He started trying to make out the words through the ink splotches.

He could make out certain words, like "Freemason" and "lodge," but then something unexpected caught his attention: the word "cipher." He peered at it for a moment, as if in shock, as if the word had a secret life of its own that no one else knew about. He tore his eyes from the paper, and then, without a second thought, he pulled out his phone and called his friend Tyler Miles. He and Bryan had worked together on numerous projects in high school and had been on the track team together years prior. Tyler was muscular and well-built; he had been a football player and a sprinter on the track team, whereas Bryan had competed in the decathlon.

Tyler was studying to be a cryptologist, a person who studies codes. Because of his special skill, his eye for detail, and his keen intellect, he could crack even the most difficult and intricate codes. But unfortunately, he had not been offered a scholarship due to the dark color of his skin, which at the time was deemed unacceptable by some, including the college admissions board. He later got in and was now top of his class.

He was not especially good with emotional situations. Even though Tyler had a steady girlfriend, Bryan was always the one who thought he was lagging behind in that treacherous relationship-battle arena. Tyler had met his girlfriend while on a visit to Israel, where she was studying Middle Eastern history as a foreign exchange student and was working with the Rothberg International School. Their relationship didn't bother Bryan, though, and he kept his head held high as Tyler stepped in the door.

He waved his hands, trying not to attract much attention to himself due to the fact that they were in a library and secretly looking for supporting documents. After all, if any one of these people who were covered in pages of text up to their eyeballs looked up and saw him, they would think he didn't belong there and was a complete idiot. Tyler walked briskly over to Bryan and gave him a hug. "How are you, my friend?" Tyler asked.

"I'm all right," Bryan replied. "Just trying to keep up with the times."

Tyler moved to the left, and Bryan could see he had brought someone else with him. "Bryan Stringer, meet Julie Ann Stratford," said Tyler.

"Nice to meet you," said Bryan.

"Julie is my fiancée," Tyler continued. "She is a DC tour guide, and as soon as I heard her speak over that megaphone, I knew she was the one for me. So, what's the problem?"

"I need a puzzle decoded," said Bryan.

"What type of puzzle?" asked Tyler.

"It's a cipher." Bryan showed him the open file with the copy of the Declaration of Independence scribbled upon with much vigor. "See, each word in the first paragraph has a circle on every other letter."

"That's because each letter that was circled comes together to make a sentence or a phrase," said Tyler. "What is this for, anyway?"

"It's a paper that I found in a yellow file in the back seat of my car after a strange man held me at gunpoint and made me drive him to the museum," said Bryan.

"What! Are you OK?" asked Tyler.

"Yes, I'm fine."

"Did you get a good look at him?"

"No," said Bryan.

"Damn! Well, let's get cracking, then."

The group started decoding the document with great anticipation as they stood around the small, curved table; Tyler circled every other letter in the rest of the first paragraph. He then took a picture of it with his phone and transferred it to his laptop and onto a digital decoding program. "This program will select all the letters I circled and then rearrange them in a certain order to make a sentence or phrase."

"So let me get this straight—you interrupted our date so you could decode a document that is like two hundred years old, from the Freemasons?" asked Julie.

"Oh, look, I found something," said Bryan excitedly.

"What is it?" asked Tyler.

"The program is done decoding the first paragraph, but it doesn't make any sense," proclaimed Bryan.

"What do you mean?" asked Tyler.

"I mean, here, look at it," said Bryan. Bryan showed Tyler the computer screen with the sentence "Outscheme brisses aliphatic Oothecae out reasoned threshers acathoid fourteen neither most dullness orientates chaliced and etamine."

"Let's just take it word by word, then," said Tyler.

"'Outscheme' is a normal phrase, so I don't think we need to understand that," exclaimed Bryan.

"'Brisses'—what does 'brisses' mean? Let's ask Google," said Tyler.

Tyler googled the word on his laptop, and the definition displayed itself on the vibrant screen. "It's a religious ceremony of male Jewish children eight days after they are born," said Tyler.

"That makes no sense, but OK," replied Bryan.

"Let's go to the next word," said Tyler. The group googled the next word, "aliphatic."

"'Aliphatic'—a compound made up of carbon atoms forming open chains," said Bryan.

"All right, next word," said Julie.

"'Oothecae,' an egg-shaped cockroach," replied Tyler.

"The next two words, 'out' and 'reasoned,' are pretty self-explanatory," said Bryan. "So let's go to the next one."

"Oh, I know this one. 'Threshers' are the wheat gatherers from like two thousand years ago who cut wheat with the grim-reaper-type things," responded Julie.

"Yes, basically," said Tyler.

"What is the next word?" asked Bryan.

"The next word is 'acathoid,'" said Julie.

The group googled the word, and the definition popped up again on Tyler's computer. "The word means skeleton or backbone," said Tyler. "I think 'fourteenth' and 'neither' and 'most,' as well as 'dullness,' are words that we all understand, right?" asked Tyler.

"Yeah, pretty straightforward," replied Julie.

"Now the last three words are a bit more complicated," said Tyler.

"'Orientates' describes a royal prince or princess getting crowned, right?" asked Bryan.

"No," said Tyler. "It says here that the word 'orientates' means the relative position of something or someone."

"The next word is 'chaliced,' which is a goblet or cup, right?" asked Julie.

"Let's see," said Tyler. Tyler googled the word to confirm Julie's supposition.

"You were right," replied Tyler.

"What about the last word?" said Bryan.

Tyler googled the word 'etamine' and looked at it with a strange expression on his face. "It says that the word 'etamine' means a light cotton or worsted fabric with an open mesh," said Tyler. "So apparently what this document is saying is that the Freemasons outschemed the Jews and cast them out. Outreasoned the Catholic Church, also known as the great harvesters of the field, to plant seeds, also known as apprentices, which are the lowest-level masons, to gain more province and influence to keep the Catholic Church in power, but while doing so, they used the Catholic Church as a testing ground to infiltrate society."

"That's ridiculous; why would they want to do that?" asked Bryan.

"To keep what they already had and gain more," said Julie.

"What does 'fourteen' mean, then?" asked Tyler.

"Well, the number fourteen normally stands for something symbolic like freedom or independence. The Freemasons liked using symbols to represent themselves," said Bryan. "Freedom and independence—freedom of religion, maybe?" asked Julie.

"Wait! Freedom of religion; that's it," said Bryan. "When the settlers in England wanted freedom in 1620, they left on the *Mayflower* for America. Because there is evidence that Freemasonry started in England in 1717, it is not necessarily plausible that Masons were on the *Mayflower* disguised as European settlers, as was once thought. But it is plausible that the stonemasons, whose origins are thought to go way back to the Middle Ages, were on the *Mayflower* and that they did come to America in 1620."

"But where does acanthoid fit in?" said Tyler.

"The definition says an acanthoid is like a spine or skeleton, so what does a spine do?" asked Bryan.

"Well, a spine is a backbone, and bones break, right?" asked Julie.

"Yeah, so?" said Bryan.

"Well, if what you said about the Freemasons liking symbolic ways of thinking is true, don't you think that a spine or bone breaking is a lot like the settlers breaking off from the Church of England?" said Tyler.

"And the Freemasons as well, right?" asked Bryan.

"Presumably yes. Even though they were gaining influence, they highly disliked the Catholic Church, so they left with the other Protestant groups to America, and there they had a place to shape their ideas and form the new country in a way that would serve their needs best," said Tyler.

"How do you know all this?" asked Bryan.

"I'm kinda into conspiracy theories," said Tyler.

Bryan nodded. "And they broke off because of their 'neither' or 'most dullness' from the church, like the cipher said."

"Yeah, and orientated or turned away from the general Church of England and general Catholicism altogether and then formed all the different Protestant religious groups, right?" said Tyler.

"Yeah, exactly," said Bryan.

"Well, what about 'chaliced' and 'etamine'?" demanded Julie.

"Well the word 'chaliced' refers to a cup or goblet," said Bryan.

"Oh my gosh; is it the Holy Grail?" asked Julie.

"Maybe," replied Bryan.

"What about the etamine?" asked Tyler.

"Well, 'etamine' means a type of fabric, so I'm guessing that it is some type of clothing or tapestry or a woven cloth of some sort," said Bryan.

"Wait, back up a minute; this first part of the cipher doesn't even make sense because there were no Jews in the United States in colonial times," said Julie.

"Well, actually a *Time* magazine article contradicted that, and it said that Jews were here in the United States before the Revolutionary War but the United States wanted Christianity to be Americanized, so since the Jews couldn't be so-called Americans, they hid them in history and covered them up with all the wars and battles they portrayed," said Tyler.

"Seriously? That's so mean," said Bryan.

"Well, that's history for ya, and we can't fix what we did in the past; all we can do is try to make a better future," said Tyler.

"Where do we go from here?" asked Julie.

"We go to the place where the Catholic Church is most prominent: Vatican City," said Bryan.

"Well, how are we going to get there?" asked Tyler.

"My dad has an apartment there—for business," replied Bryan.

"Oh yeah, I forgot your family's rich," said Tyler.

"Not rich—fortunate. And think of it as a free trip," replied Bryan.

CHAPTER 2
EMPTY PIECES

The group took a plane flight to Vatican City two days after. Using Bryan's dad's frequent-flier miles, they were able to go there with almost no expense. The group was walking down a dark, gray street leading into the city. "I can't believe I had to miss my next presentation for this," said Bryan.

"Well, relax, everything will work out," said Julie.

"Stop worrying about him; you'll only make him more stressed," said Tyler.

"I'm not stressed," replied Bryan.

"Oh, really? Then is that why you look all crinkly, wrinkly, and depressed?" asked Julie.

"What? No, I look fine," said Bryan.

"You look like a tourist," said Julie.

"You do look like a tourist," said Tyler in agreement.

"Well, you guys clearly have no taste," replied Bryan.

"If you think khakis and a blue polo look good together, you are sadly mistaken," said Julie.

"Well, at least he isn't wearing a Hawaiian shirt and a Polaroid camera around his neck." Tyler chuckled.

"OK, OK, stop it, you two; you aren't on your honey-moon just yet, and besides, we have to blend in. And just to let you know, I would look awesome in a Hawaiian shirt." Bryan flipped up his collar, and Julie and Tyler looked at Bryan and then at each other, determining if they should say something about Bryan's newfound swagger; they decided to keep the thought to themselves. Eventually they followed Bryan into Saint Peter's Square. "How could you even afford this flight?" asked Tyler.

"There is a thing called travel miles," said Bryan.

The group walked around the marvelous circular structure with its massive white stone and marble col-umns. They looked up at all the incredible white stat-ues above them, gazing down upon them. As the group moved inward, they saw the massively tall, tan Egyptian obelisk grounded firmly within the center of the large curricular area peered upon by millions.

"So what do we need to do here exactly?" asked Julie.

"Well, the first part of the cipher said that the Freemasons were reasoning with the Catholic Church to keep its power, so what we have to do is to find evi-dence that they were doing that and figure out why the Freemasons were then kicked out of the Catholic Church," said Bryan.

"Where are we going to find that here?" asked Julie.

"The Vatican Archive," said Tyler.

"We can't just walk right into the Vatican Archive, and besides, they only let, like, sixty people at a time go in there, and you have to have an introductory letter from a prestigious college or university indicating you are doing research," said Julie.

"Got a letter right here from a Dr. Simmons from Yale," said Tyler.

"How did you get that?" asked Julie.

"I swiped it from an old email from about five years back, printed it out yesterday, and bash, boom, bang, here we are!"

"OK, but we still would need to be doing some type of research," said Julie.

"We are here to study the pope's history because we will ostensibly be writing a thesis paper on him; that is our reason for being here," said Bryan.

"I can't believe it; I just can't believe it! We are going to go into one of the world's greatest historical time capsules, one dating back to the origin of one of the most popular religions in the world," said Julie.

The group walked up the cold, hard yellow stone steps, their feet pushing off from each step with swiftness and overwhelming courage, until they reached the top of the heavy slabs of unbroken stone. The tall white gates of the archive were closed before them, and it seemed like more and more people were swarming in like angered bees. Soon, at around 8:30 a.m., the locked gates were opened with precision and finesse from the religious faculty that guarded the precious keys. Once the many gates were open, the group was allowed to enter with their passports and the letter from Tyler. Everything seemed to be going according to plan.

"Passport and letter of introduction, please," said the guard at the main gate. The guard patted them each down and continued, "You are all clear. Please leave your things in a compartment over on the left. There are no pictures permitted. Have a nice day."

They left all their things on the left side of the entry in a cubby-like compartment and continued to the archive. All Bryan had in his pocket was a yellow glow stick he had found on the ground, a note card, a small pencil, and fifty euros. Tyler and Julie left everything from their pockets in the cubby area.

The group entered the vast archive of old, carefully bound documents and religious texts and manuscripts, which had only ever been seen by very few. A curator walked the small group back to a room where walls covered with shelves held old, cryptic-looking documents and six long, rectangular wooden tables and twelve chairs had been placed in the center of the room. "Which documents are you looking for today?" the curator asked.

"We are looking for documents from around 1730; the subject matter is Freemasons and the church," said Bryan.

"All right, I will be right back with your documents, sir," said the curator. The curator returned to the room ten minutes later with a small stack of documents.

"Here is everything we have on the Freemasons and the church; I hope you find what you are looking for," said the curator. Bryan nodded and smiled, and the curator left the room. Bryan and his colleagues looked through each document with precision and extreme care and effort so as to not miss a thing.

"It says here that the Freemasons were kicked out of the church because their Masonic principles and rituals misrepresented and were irreconcilable with the Catholic doctrines," said Bryan. Bryan held the document up to the light and realized that there were lightly tinted numbers under the handwritten words. "Look, look here, see these numbers."

"I don't see any numbers," said Julie. Bryan pulled out his yellow glow stick from his pocket and put it on the document under the row of faded numbers.

"Oh, I sort of see them now," said Julie.

"Write them out so I can see," said Tyler. Bryan held the document up to the light with one hand and wrote the numbers down on the note card: "17, 33, 12, 24, 15, 2."

The group intensely examined the numbers, trying to make some sense out of them. "Maybe these numbers correspond to a vault or safe combination code," said Tyler.

"No, I don't think so because one, they didn't have safes in the 1730s, and two, this combination would be too long," said Bryan.

"What could they mean?" asked Julie.

The group looked at the document again. "Wait, there's something else here; it's backward and upside down," exclaimed Tyler. "Quick, ask the curator for a mirror."

Bryan ran to get the curator and asked for a mirror. The curator brought them a small rectangular mirror and stayed to see what they might find until Bryan gave her a look of "please leave," and she then left the room once more. Bryan, Tyler, and Julie read the fated sentence together: "Trust the tapestry; the resurrection is near."

"What in the heck does that mean?" asked Tyler.

"I don't know," declared Bryan.

"OK, let's just focus on the numbers for now," said Julie.

The group looked over the list of numbers again on the small piece of paper Bryan had written them on minutes earlier. And once again the trio tried to break the code placed before them. "Let's just take the first number, number seventeen," said Julie. "What does the number seventeen represent to the Freemasons?"

The group paced back and forth across the room with extreme composure and diligence, trying to unravel the complex puzzles swirling in their minds. "The Freemasons have these things called degrees, which are levels or steps to becoming better men, and they go up to thirty-three, and then you go to a certain temple called the Scottish Rite, and you go higher up the levels," said Bryan.

"Why is it called the Scottish Rite?" asked Julie.

"I don't actually know, but what I do know is that is where the higher Masons go for secret meetings and to discuss their secret agendas," said Bryan.

"Well, maybe the number corresponds with a temple they have," said Tyler.

"Wait! Read me those numbers again," said Bryan.

Tyler read the numbers aloud. "Uh. OK. Seventeen, thirty-three, twelve."

"Wait, stop, go back one," said Bryan.

"Twelve?" asked Tyler.

"No, no, back one more," said Bryan.

"Seventeen, thirty-three," said Tyler.

"Yes that's it—1733" replied Bryan.

"What have you figured out?" asked Tyler excitedly.

"Well, this may not be right, but 1733 is the street address of the Masonic temple in Washington, DC," said Bryan.

"Well, that's as good a place to start as any," said Julie.

"Let's go, then," said Tyler.

The group left, packed their things, and caught the first plane back to DC.

* * *

The Scottish Rite Supreme Council Temple building, 1733 Sixteenth Street, Washington, DC, two days after Vatican City

Bryan, Tyler, and Julie were across the street from the Freemason temple, talking to one another.

"How do you want to approach this?" asked Julie.

"Well, my plan is to go in with a tourist group and then break off into the main library and see where we will go from there," said Bryan.

"Um, I have a question—what if we get caught?" asked Tyler.

"Well, if we get caught, we do the one thing we do best," said Bryan.

"What is that?" asked Tyler.

"Run!" replied Bryan.

"Oh, great plan," Tyler said sarcastically.

"I kind of like it; it's daring yet treacherous," said Julie.

"Stop encouraging him," demanded Tyler.

"If I'm going to get caught, I want to be caught doing something worthwhile," said Julie.

"Sure," Tyler replied sarcastically.

"OK, everybody clear on the plan?" asked Bryan. They all nodded. "Great."

The group intermingled with a tour group and began to walk up the big white stone steps of the temple. "Were we supposed to bring holy sacrifices?" Tyler jokingly whispered.

"What? Shhh," whispered Bryan.

The group entered the building and walked into the vast atrium. One of the ladies who led the tour came up to the leader of our tourist group and asked if they had a tour scheduled, and the leader of our tourist group said they had one scheduled for eleven thirty. Bryan glanced down at his watch. It was 11:28. Tyler and Julie tried to mix in with the tourist group and stay out of sight so as to not get spotted by the leader of their tourist group or the tour participants, most of whom seemed to know one another.

Those two long minutes felt like an eternity, but as soon as they got the tour started, the trio was able to blend in so as not to be recognized. The tour guide led them up a flight of stairs in the back of the building. As Bryan went up the steps, he felt the curved gold metal railing on each side of the white marble stairs and fixed his eyes on a bronze bust of Albert Pike. They then turned and went up a second flight of stairs and entered the temple room. The temple room had eighteen small red tables and chairs on either side.

In the center was an altar with a purple padded center, and on it were nine books ostensibly used for initiations and gatherings. The Freemasons only had initiations a few times a year. It puzzled Bryan, though, that they would have a massive building like this to use only a few times every year. It seemed a little suspicious. He thought about it while they exited the temple room and entered a hallway leading to the George Washington Banquet Hall.

Tyler, Julie, and Bryan left the tourist group and quickly walked into the main library. The main library was big but not as big and spread out as the Library of Congress. This library had triple sets of brown curved double doors, each with an oval-shaped window. The walls were covered with dark-brown shelves up to the ceiling, and it was said to have every book on Freemasonry ever recorded. The room was empty, which was good, but it left a lot of empty space to look.

"Where do we start?" asked Tyler.

"Well, the number code brought us here; maybe it has something to do with what we do next," said Julie.

"What are the next numbers?" asked Tyler.

Bryan glanced down at the small piece of paper he had written the numbers on earlier. "The next numbers are twelve, twenty-four, fifteen, and two," said Bryan.

"What could twelve be?" wondered Julie.

"Well, there's a shelf that says twelve above it right here," said Tyler.

Bryan and Julie looked up to see that all the brown bookcases had numbers plated and indented in gold above each of them, from one to twelve.

The group went over to the twelfth shelf. "What now?" asked Julie.

"Just start looking," said Bryan. With great determination, the group looked though book after book on the shelf and then put each book quickly back on the shelf.

"Wait," said Julie abruptly.

"What?" Bryan exclaimed.

"The numbers are steps," said Julie.

"What do you mean?" asked Bryan.

"Well, the number seventeen thirty-three led us here, and the number twelve led us to the shelf, so the next number, twenty-four, must have something to do with a book on the shelf," said Julie.

"You're probably right," said Tyler.

"What could it mean then, twelfth book, twelfth page?" said Bryan.

"All of the above?" questioned Julie.

The group once again dug though the twelfth book, the twelfth pages of books, and the twelfth paragraphs and lines in every book in every shelf.

"It has to be here—what are we missing?" Bryan sighed.

"OK. Let's all step back and take a deep breath," said Tyler. The group stepped away from the shelf and took a breath. Tyler continued, "OK, what are we trying to find?

"We are trying to find something relating to the number twelve, and it is supposed to be connected to Freemasonry," said Bryan.

"What do we think is connecting the bookshelf to Freemasonry?" asked Julie.

"Duh, the number twelve from the document we found in the Vatican Archives," said Tyler.

"So there must be something in this bookshelf that is connected to the other letters, right?" asked Julie.

"Well, yes, but we don't know what it is yet," said Bryan.

"OMG. Can we please get over the obvious and focus on the problem at hand!" exclaimed Tyler.

"We're trying to think through a problem, Tyler; calm down and stop being so hotheaded!" replied Bryan.

Tyler walked away furious from the others and put his head down and hands on his neck, about to explode with frustration and anger from the stress caused by Bryan's remark. He turned around. "What do you want me to do? You led us here on this stupid, meaningless clue-hunting charade that will lead to nowhere!" exclaimed Tyler in fury.

"I did not lead you into a charade, Tyler. There is something here; I know it. All I want you to do is help us solve this puzzle," replied Bryan in a firm tone.

Tyler took a deep breath in and let go of his frustration. "OK, what do we do next?"

"First, let's just all relax and take a breath and realize that we're not in a Dan Brown novel. The ending isn't written yet. And realize that these clues are a lot more complicated than any book because this is real life. We need to find a way to connect the number twelve to the bookshelf or something else, but I don't see any other number twelves, so I guess it is this one," said Bryan.

"Hey, has anyone really looked at the next number, twenty-four, and connected it to a book on the shelf?" asked Julie.

"What is the book's title?" asked Bryan.

"*The Constitutions of the Freemasons*," said Julie.

"Seriously?" asked Bryan.

"Yeah, seriously. Why? Do you know it?" asked Julie.

"Yeah; it was written and printed by James Anderson in 1723."

"Who is James Anderson?" asked Tyler.

"James Anderson was a Scottish writer and minister. He wrote this document, and only about one hundred were printed, and only a few remain, including one here, in the Scottish Rite Council library."

"OK, so let's say we have the right document; now what?" said Tyler.

"The next number," said Julie.

"The next numbers are fifteen and two," said Bryan.

"Fifteenth paragraph, maybe?" asked Tyler.

"And the second sentence," said Bryan.

Julie flipped though the document and found the fifteenth paragraph and the second sentence and read it out loud: "'It being seven thousand seven hundred feet on a compass.'"

"What in the heck does that mean?" exclaimed Tyler.

Bryan then saw a familiar face in the small oval window on one of the brown doors. It was the man who had held a gun to his head in his car four days earlier. "Everyone, go! Go! We have to go now!" Bryan yelled with panic in his voice. Bryan took hold of their arms and yanked the other members of the group forward.

"Shhh, Bryan, we're in a library!" exclaimed Julie, holding one finger up to her mouth.

Bryan tilted his head to the side and gave Julie a look of annoyance.

"Ugh, Bryan, stop pulling on my arm; what are you doing!" exclaimed Julie.

"Chill, bro, OK? Nobody needs to be pulled like that," exclaimed Tyler.

"You see that man outside the door, with the bald head and big muscles? Well, he was the guy who held a gun to my head," said Bryan.

"You mean in your car?" asked Tyler.

"Yes, in my car," replied Bryan.

"Are you sure?" asked Julie.

"I am eighty-five percent sure," said Bryan.

"Well, that's reassuring," replied Tyler.

"Wait, I found something else," Julie exclaimed.

"What is it?" Bryan asked.

"It's a short sentence in the book on the fifteenth page right next to the inside book binding," Julie said.

"What does it say?" asked Tyler.

"It says, 'Trust the tapestry; the resurrection is near,'" said Julie.

"OK, cool; now can we get out of here!" Bryan exclaimed.

The group went out through the farthest brown door to the right and walked down the stone steps and left the Masonic temple with a sense of urgency. They went back to Bryan's house to try to figure out what the phrase meant. It was a small one-story white house with gray shingles and a side-tilted roof.

The group went inside, and Julie and Tyler sat down at the wood dining table adjacent to the kitchen as Bryan brought out some chips and drinks. Julie placed the fifteenth page of the book, which she had torn out, on the table.

Bryan wheeled a large whiteboard in front of the table and began writing the words seen on page 15: "Trust the tapestry; the resurrection is near." "What does this mean?" said Bryan as he underlined the sentence on the board.

"I think we should break it down," said Julie.

"That's a great idea, babe," said Tyler.

"Thanks, babe," said Julie.

"OK, OK, break it up, you two. We have a mystery to solve. You can finish your mushiness and making me feel awkward when we're finished solving the mystery. OK? Thank you," said Bryan.

"Somebody's jealous," whispered Tyler across the table to Julie.

"I heard that!" snapped Bryan.

The group got to work to solving the riddle. "OK, the first part of the phrase—'Trust the tapestry.'" said Bryan.

"Since it was a phrase taken from the law of the Masons, could it be talking about a Masonic tapestry? I know they created those during the medieval era."

"OK, OK, Masonic tapestries—what do we know?" asked Bryan.

"I know absolutely nothing," said Tyler.

"I can't help you; most of the tapestries I know of were made in the Renaissance," said Julie.

"What did you just say?" asked Bryan.

"I said that I can't help you because all the tapestries I know are from the Renaissance."

"The Renaissance—that's it!" exclaimed Bryan.

"Wait, I don't understand," said Julie.

"Yeah, neither do I," said Tyler.

"Well, in the Renaissance there were painters, sculptors, inventors; the Renaissance was a rebirth of ideas and skills marked by people working together against the Catholic Church, who had cast out science and logical reasoning for religion and spirituality," said Bryan.

"And...please get to the point," said Tyler.

"Well, these men, these thinkers, created small groups and societies like the Illuminati and yes, the Freemasons, and the church didn't like that, so they burned people at the stake. So the societies were forced to go underground, and that's why we now call them secret societies," said Bryan.

"OK, that's great and all, except for the burning part, but when are we going to get to the tapestry?" asked Tyler.

"In a minute," announced Bryan. "Now these secret societies were creating the most famous works of art before they went underground, and one of them was called the *Resurrection of Christ*. It was weaved by one of the greatest minds of the Renaissance, Raphael."

"Wait, you mean to tell me that this book is telling us that a fourteenth-century painter was actually a Freemason?" asked Tyler.

"Well, they didn't call it that at that time but yes, basically," said Bryan.

"Oh my God," whispered Julie.

"Where is it? Can we go get it?" asked Tyler.

"Yes, we can; it's back in the Vatican," said Bryan.

"Where in the Vatican?" asked Tyler.

"The Vatican again? We just got back," responded Julie, whining.

"The Vatican Museum. And I know we just got back, but there's only one problem," said Bryan.

"What is that?" exclaimed Tyler.

"To see it is one thing, but we are going to have to steal it," said Bryan.

Julie perked up out of her tired state, and the two boys knew she was perfectly fine going back after hearing that comment. "I'm not going back!" said Julie in a harsh tone.

CHAPTER 3
SCOUTING OUT

After Bryan and Tyler at long last persuaded Julie, the group took a plane flight back to Vatican City. They walked down the streets of the Vatican again. "So if the book was leading us back to the Vatican, it must have been important, right?" asked Tyler.

"You're right; it must be showing us that since the Freemasons were kicked out of the church, the Freemasons revolted by using their art to insult them through paintings, sculptures, and—before you ask—yes, tapestries," said Bryan.

"So this tapestry is supposed to lead us to what? What is this whole thing all about? The decoration, the numbers, the book—everything has to lead to something, right? It can't just be a wild-goose chase, right?" asked Bryan.

"Well, it could be, in which case we basically wasted money, time, and resources for something that doesn't really exist, so let's just hope it leads to something," said Bryan.

"What if Tyler is right? What if it doesn't lead to anything? Then we are basically screwed," Julie said dejectedly.

"Yeah, so let's just pray that we are on the right track," Bryan said, trying to encourage them.

"I think that this country is changing you, Bryan," Tyler said quietly.

"Oh, really? How so?" asked Bryan.

"Well, you just said, 'Let's pray,' and you're not religious," Tyler replied.

"You don't know that I'm not religious. You just assume, and assumptions are the downfall of man," Bryan said, sounding very annoyed.

"So are you or are you not religious?" Julie said.

"Well I am, but I'm not," said Bryan.

"What do you mean?" asked Tyler.

"Well, I don't necessarily believe in the Catholic idea of relics and traditions like Mary, but I do believe in something bigger than us," Bryan said thoughtfully.

The group walked up to the entrance of the Vatican Museum. A guard met them at the door and asked them to pay the price of admission. "Entrance fee, eight euros per person, please, and then please step forward for metal detection," the guard said. The group walked forward and lined up to go through the metal detector.

Bryan looked up at the tall, wide arch before them and thought it appeared like an entrance to another world. He stepped forward a few more feet to get scanned again by the black-and-yellow wand waving in front of his body. The officer let the group pass one by one through the checkpoint, and they walked through the arch into a massive corridor covered with endless wall paintings and large white marble sculptures. As they ventured farther and farther into the vast catacombs of the museum, they eventually arrived at the Hall of Tapestries.

"So why are there so many tapestries in this hall?" asked Julie.

"Well, the Hall of Tapestries basically takes a person through twelve uniquely woven stories of Jesus's life," Bryan answered.

"So were all of these created by Raphael?" asked Julie.

"Yes, they were all created by Raphael and his students and originally hung in the Sistine Chapel but were eventually taken down." Bryan replied.

"How do you know so much about these things?" asked Julie.

"Well, my parents raised me Catholic," said Bryan.

"Oh, so you were religious; you just aren't religious now?" queried Tyler.

"Yes, my parents were Catholic, but I broke away from Catholicism because to me it was just rules and laws, and from my point of view, the Catholic Church had just moved away from the thing that made Christianity special and became a politicized, highly controversial religion of tradition and sacred material relics of the Virgin Mary and basically worshiping the pope instead of God and not harnessing true faith. They are missing the whole part of Christianity. Christianity isn't necessarily a religion; it's a one-on-one relationship with the one who created you," said Bryan.

"Well, what about the one billion Catholics in the world? Are you saying that they are wrong for believing in Catholicism?" asked Julie.

"People can believe what they want to believe, but at the end of the day, you have to realize and justify the facts, and the truth is that I don't believe in Jesus because he was a great man or because of all the miracles he has done or because my parents brought me to Mass every Sunday. I believe in Jesus and Christianity just because it is simply true," said Bryan.

The group continued down the Hall of Tapestries, marveling at the vibrant colors and epic stories the tapestries held within their five-hundred-year-old worn fabrics, which had been meticulously woven together into intricate patterns. Tyler, Bryan, and Julie stopped at the tapestry depicting the resurrection of Christ and tried to take it all in. The tapestry was a large rectangular shape depicting soldiers with faces full of fear as they watched Jesus coming out of the tomb wearing a red robe with his hands and feet pierced from the nails of the Crucifixion.

"Is it really true that Jesus survived the Crucifixion?" asked Julie.

"There is no way in hell that any man would be able to survive such excruciating pain on a rotting piece of wood and be in a tomb three days buried," said Tyler.

"Well," Julie said, "I think Jesus was just a man and wasn't fully dead, just half dead, and he used the three days in the tomb to recuperate from the Roman torture trap. Did anyone see a back entrance to the tomb? Maybe Mary Magdalene helped nurse Jesus back to health."

"Oh, so you're going the Jesus bloodline route, like in *The Da Vinci Code*?" asked Tyler.

"Listen, you guys can think what you want of it. I am sticking to my belief system, and besides, we have a real mystery on our hands, not one based on historical fiction," said Bryan. "What are we even looking for?" asked Julie.

A tour guide walked by and overheard the question. "Can I help you?" the tour guide asked in English with an Italian accent.

"Well, we are trying to connect the tapestry to a historical treasure or event," said Tyler.

"Oh. Treasure." The tour guide chuckled a little, trying to contain her laughter because of the odd, childish question. "It has been said to be secretly and historically connected to the ark of the covenant."

"Why is that?" asked Bryan.

"Well, the ark was supposedly connected to the tomb by way of the town of Emmaus, where the ark of the covenant stood and where Jesus walked after his resurrection," said the tour guide.

"Oh, OK, thank you," said Bryan.

"You're very welcome. I hope you enjoy the rest of the Vatican Museum."

The tour guide continued her tour with another group while Bryan, Tyler, and Julie tried to uncover the puzzle that was deeply embedded in the tapestry. "So if the tour guide is right, then what are the Freemasons hiding in the ark of the covenant?" asked Julie.

"I don't think they are hiding something in the ark; I think they have the ark and are protecting it," said Tyler.

"What do you mean?" asked Bryan.

"Well, it's just a theory, but what if the Freemasons are protecting the ark of the covenant?" said Tyler.

"Why would they be protecting it? I thought that they disliked Christianity because the Catholic Church cast them out," said Bryan.

"Well, normally the ark is guarded by one singular individual, like a monk. So what if the monk in charge of guarding the ark is actually a Freemason and is secretly guarding the ark for the Freemasons to use," said Tyler.

"That actually seems plausible," said Bryan.

"But for what purpose?" asked Julie.

"I don't know," replied Bryan with a puzzled look on his face. "It has to have something to do with the tapestry. Why else would the book lead us here?"

"You may be right!" Julie said excitedly. "There has to be something here!"

Bryan and Tyler looked carefully again at the tapestry as Julie paced back and forth in front of it, noting that there was something strange about the tapestry. "Look at Jesus's eyes in the tapestry," said Julie.

"Yeah, what about them?" asked Bryan.

"They're following me," exclaimed Julie.

"What? How?" asked Tyler.

"I don't know," said Julie.

"It seems to be some type of optical illusion," said Bryan.

"That's crazy," said Tyler. "So where do we go from here?"

"I don't know, but we're going to have to examine it more closely," said Bryan.

"How are we supposed to do that? It's not like we can take it off the wall," said Tyler. "Maybe we can," said Bryan with a knowing look in his eyes.

The group left the Vatican Museum and went back to Bryan's dad's apartment. They entered the small gray stone building and went up to the second floor, where the one-bedroom apartment was located. The apartment consisted of a bedroom conjoined with a living room and tiny kitchenette with a white retro mini fridge and metal circular fireplace. The group went into the living room, and Tyler and Julie sat down on a white couch, while Bryan sat adjacent to them on a white chair after he had brought out some cheese and wine and set it on a rectangular wooden table in the middle of the room.

"How are we going to examine the tapestry more closely?" asked Tyler.

"Were going to have to steal it," said Bryan.

"What! Steal it! Are you insane?" asked Julie incredulously. Julie got up and started pacing around the room. "This is absolutely ridiculous! How are we supposed to steal the tapestry?"

Tyler said excitedly, "We could do sort of what they did in *National Treasure* and spill something on it so it will have to go into cleaning, and that's when we strike."

"No," Bryan said quickly. "Whatever we spilled on it could damage the tapestry, and if we stole it like that, then they would know it was missing, and then they would shut down the Vatican."

Julie responded, "You are right. Plus, the Vatican has its own police force, and when it's shut down, the place is impenetrable inside and out."

"We could use the catacombs under the city," suggested Tyler.

"Oh, that reminds me," said Bryan as he opened his brown leather duffel bag and grabbed a roll of blueprints. He unrolled the blueprints on the table and placed metal pins on opposite ends of the blueprints to hold them down.

"Where did you get these?" asked Tyler, pointing at the blueprints.

"The internet. Google has tons of maps and blueprints of Vatican City and the museum," answered Bryan. "So here is my plan: Vatican City is point five miles wide, so I say we go to the left of Saint Peter's Square, because that's the closest point to the museum. There will be guards posted around the clock at the front of the museum and inside the wall but not on the outside of the wall. Therefore we would need to time our ascent and descent to avoid the guards."

"Wait," Tyler interrupted, pointing to a section of the blueprint. "Why don't we just scale the tops of the roofs of these buildings here?"

"Hold on," said Bryan. "The top of the Gate of Saint Pellegrino leads to the residence of the pope and the Vatican bank."

Bryan was cut off by Julie. "And then we go around the top of the bank and continue onto the roof of the residence of the pope and then finally to the roof of the museum!"

"Exactly," replied Bryan, "but we would still have to go around to the side of Borgia Tower because that is the side where the tapestries are held. So all we would have to do is cut through the roof, repel down into the Hall of Tapestries, get the tapestry, and then raise it up to the roof with the rope we repelled down with, and then, *boom*, we scale the building again and we are home free."

"But there's only one problem: How do we get them to not notice the tapestry is gone?" asked Julie.

"Simple, we switch it," said Bryan.

"Switch it? Switch it with what?" asked Tyler.

"A copy," said Bryan.

"There is no way we would be able to find an exact replica of the resurrection of Jesus tapestry," said Julie.

"I know a guy," said Bryan mysteriously.

Julie laughed. "You know someone who sells authentic Vatican tapestries?"

"Well, he can get anything you want, really," said Bryan.

* * *

The group traveled a short distance down a few cobblestone streets until they saw a man leaning against a wall with one leg propped up against it. "Is that who we are meeting with?" asked Julie in a scared, squeaky voice.

"Yeah. Why? Are you scared?" asked Bryan.

"What! No. I am a strong independent women," said Julie with confidence.

"Good. You'll need to be," said Bryan.

"Wait, you're not independent, though—you're with me," said Tyler.

Julie gave him a dirty look. "Just because I'm dating you doesn't mean I can't have my own life, but I do love you."

Bryan interrupted them. "You're digging yourself into a hole that you might not be able to get out of." Julie chuckled and grabbed hold of Tyler's hand and put her head on his shoulder as they walked the final few feet up to the unsuspecting figure leaning up against the wall.

"Ah, Stringer, how are you? It's been a while, my friend," said the mysterious figure. The man was in his midforties and had big bags under his eyes. His Italian accent mixed with English sounded to Julie and Tyler just like a slur of meaningless words.

"Gwardo! I haven't seen you since the Taste of Roma Festival! Ah, was it 2012?"

Gwardo laughed. "That's it! You were just a young runt then.

"I remember you were scouting out a painting of ours for your client, and we caught you at our villa," said Bryan.

"Ah, but then you convinced your dad to let me go." Gwardo laughed.

"That's why you owe me."

"Yeah, yeah, don't remind me."

Bryan gave Gwardo a friendly slap on the back as he introduced him to his friends. Bryan very quickly whispered his plans to steal the tapestry to Gwardo. "Do you think it will work?" he asked hopefully.

"Getting in seems fine, but getting out is the problem; give me a couple of days to think of a plan."

Bryan agreed. The group went and saw all Italy had to offer, including some of its famous landmarks, and it felt like they ate endless meals. Then, after a few days, Gwardo called, and the group went back to the street where they had first met him.

"What you want to do is this: Once you cut through the roof and are on the floor, you will see doors at both ends of the hall. Plug each keyhole with putty so that if something goes wrong, you can delay the guards and give yourself more time.

"Then, instead of going back out through the roof, cut through the floor and go down into the catacombs. This map will show you the way through the catacombs, and I will be waiting with the van, but come, we will have to practice," whispered Gwardo conspiratorially.

The group traveled to Gwardo's inner-city apartment. The apartment was a bit run-down, with broken shingles and some paint peeling on the inside. Bryan saw a circular saw on the table along with Dexpan, which is designed to break up flooring.

"Try it," said Gwardo. "The Dexpan will break down the floor, which will enable you to saw through it easily.

Bryan started the process. "No, no," said Gwardo. "You have to cut a groove in the floor the shape and size you need, then put Dexpan in the cracks; then it will slowly break up the floor while you are cutting."

Bryan followed Gwardo's instructions, and like a broken bar of soap, the concrete cracked, and the flooring fell through. "Wow!" Bryan exclaimed excitedly.

"I think you're ready," said Gwardo.

* * *

Three days later the three twenty-two-year-olds waited for Gwardo outside his apartment. "Do you have it?" asked Bryan.

"It's in the van around the corner. It took me forever to make; I had to get seven other people to help me due to the crunched time frame," said Gwardo, handing Bryan the keys. "By the way, I want the real tapestry when you're finished with it."

"Why?" asked Julie.

"No tapestry, no help," said Gwardo menacingly.

"Fine," Bryan replied reluctantly.

"*Grazie.* May God protect you and keep you safe," said Gwardo as he shook Bryan's hand.

"Blessings to you, my friend," said Bryan.

The group walked up the street, and as they turned the corner, a long white sprinter van came into sight. Bryan opened one of the back doors, peering at a long tapestry rolled up and in a plastic seal. Bryan also saw a diamond circular saw with an extra blade, as well as black rope, harnesses, and carabiners. Lying to the side was a small automatic winch and three black outfits.

Bryan quickly shut the back door of the van and walked up to the driver's-side door and got in with his friends. "So who exactly was that guy? I still don't understand him," said Julie. "His name is Gwardo; he's a fence. We met at a festival when I was around twelve or thirteen," said Bryan.

"I don't like him," said Julie, wrinkling up her nose. "He's sketchy."

"Well, he's a fence, so that's kinda what you get, and besides, he gave us what we needed, so that's all that matters," said Bryan.

The group drove to the outer left wall of Vatican City, parked the van, and waited till midnight. The group got changed into black outfits.

"What do we do now? We have like two hours," said Julie.

"You wanna make out?" asked Tyler. Julie gave Tyler a look of "I can't believe you just said that," and Tyler instantly realized what a dumb question that was because Bryan was right there. To save his skin, he said, "You wanna play Uno?" Tyler held up a deck of cards.

"Sure, let's play Uno," said Julie. "You wanna play?" she asked Bryan.

"No, I'm going to take a walk and survey the street," replied Bryan in a semisour tone.

Bryan got out of the van and shut the door and began to walk down the street. "I'm going to go talk to him," said Julie.

"Julie, come on, relax and let him walk; it's part of his process," said Tyler, but Julie was already out of the van and walking toward Bryan.

"Bryan, wait up!" yelled Julie. Bryan stopped and allowed Julie to catch up, and then the two walked side by side through the dark of night. "Hey, you, OK?"

Bryan sighed and then replied, "Why can't I have what you two have?"

"What? A relationship?" asked Julie.

"Yes, a relationship. I feel like all the girls don't like me that way just because I'm different," said Bryan.

"Bryan you're not different; you're just special. We're all special in our own ways. I mean, look at Tyler. He has his own quirks and strange things, which I have to put up with, but we're each so different and special. And I mean, different is good, and special is good, and eventually you will find that other person who loves you for the special person you are. It all just takes time; you can't rush love, Bryan."

"Yeah, I guess so."

"Can we go back to the van now?"

"Sure."

The two walked back to the van and opened the door to find Tyler playing Uno by himself. They joined him.

"You OK, bud?" asked Tyler.

"Yeah, I just needed some air," said Bryan.

"Well, guess what I found out while you two were gone? I found out that it is literally impossible to play Uno by yourself," said Tyler.

"What time is it?" asked Julie.

"It's five minutes till midnight," said Tyler.

"Let's get ready, then," replied Julie.

"Let me just call Gwardo to come pick up the van after we're over the wall," said Bryan. "And let's get ready to steal the most valuable tapestry in existence."

CHAPTER 4

THE HEIST

Bryan, Julie, and Tyler got out of the van and threw a rope with a hook above the wall. Tyler pulled on it to make sure it would hold. Bryan began the climb; with his feet up against the outside wall and the winch attached to his back, he swiftly climbed to the top of the east wall. He attached the winch to the wall and quietly said to the people below, "OK, I attached the electric winch, so now you can attach the dolly to the cable." Julie attached the dolly with the welding tools to the winch and gave Bryan the thumbs-up.

The electric winch lifted the welding tools up high in the air until they reached Bryan. Bryan grabbed the handle of the dolly and pulled it over the side of the wall to the small wooden scaffolding where he was standing and unclipped the big black metal hook and sent the hook back down. "OK, we're good! Send up the tapestry," said Bryan. Once again Julie and Tyler signaled Bryan from the ground.

The winch lowered, and Julie and Tyler grabbed the massive tapestry duplicate from the van and carried it over their shoulders, then placed it on the ground. Tyler then went and grabbed two one-yard-long steel cables from the back of the van and slid each cable under the rolled-up tapestry. He folded the strands of steel around each side and capped each side off with a thick zip tie, connecting each end. Julie then wove a longer five-yard cable of the same thickness in between both steel loops on each end, creating an open metal barred cage for the duplicate tapestry. Then Tyler and Julie connected the longer steel cable to the winch's hook and gave Bryan the signal to raise it.

Bryan grabbed the tapestry duplicate with both hands and hurled it over the rest of the wall and onto the scaffolding. Tyler and Julie climbed the black rope, one after the other, much like Bryan had done before. "This reminds me of gym class," said Tyler.

"This is so much easier compared to cheer and doing upper-body workouts," replied Julie.

After about two minutes, the group was once again together, over the wall and on the scaffolding. Gwardo was on the ground next to the van, and Bryan gave him the signal to drive the van to the catacombs to pick them up. Bryan and Tyler then carried the false tapestry over their shoulders, single file, while Julie handled the dolly welding equipment. The group then walked across the tops of the barracks of the Swiss Guard.

Bryan and Tyler were being very quiet, trying not to make much noise because they didn't want to alert the Swiss Guard. Julie had the much harder task of keeping the rusty wheels of the dolly from squeaking. *Squeak*— the wheels of the dolly kept squeaking along the rooftop.

"Can you shut that thing up!" declared Bryan quietly so as to not awaken the security guards below them. Suddenly, without warning, a spotlight panned around from a nearby building. Tyler and Bryan hit the top of the roof when dropping on their stomach to avoid the spotlight, but Julie was too focused on her dolly situation to notice.

"Julie, hit the deck!" exclaimed Tyler quietly, with concern in his voice. Julie quickly laid the dolly down and lay down on the roof herself. The bright white light of the spotlight quickly shined over them and then back again. About a minute later, the spotlight turned off, and the gang looked around and then quietly got up and continued on. Once they got to the place where they were above the gate of Saint Pellegrino, they stopped and stared in awe at what lay before them.

The gate was thin and metal. Bryan squatted down and felt the gate to see if it would move if he stood on it. The gate wobbled a bit back and forth, but it wasn't too bad. "What do we do now?" asked Tyler.

"We can't possibly cross that; the gate is too thin," said Julie.

"It'll be just like a catwalk," said Bryan.

Tyler and Bryan begin the walk with the false tapestry in their hands. "All right, slow and steady," said Bryan. Tyler and Bryan's legs were shaking violently as the two walked across the top of the metal gate. They finally got across, and now it was Julie's turn.

"What do I do? I don't know how to do this!" exclaimed Julie.

"Just take it one step at a time. Here, to make it easier, hand us the dolly," said Bryan. Julie leaned over and held out the metal dolly with one hand and used her other hand to support the back of the metal mammoth. Bryan reached out on the other side, with Tyler holding on to him so he wouldn't fall. Bryan barely grabbed the other end of the dolly and reached farther for a better grasp.

"Bryan, I can't hold on to you!" said Tyler.

"I've almost got it." exclaimed Bryan. Bryan had a full grasp on it now and pulled it in toward his chest. With his momentum going backward due to the weight of the green gas tank duct-taped to the dolly, Bryan was propelled on top of Tyler, and they both fell to the ground.

"Aw, man," said Tyler, half conscious.

"Man, that dolly is heavy," declared Bryan.

"You boys OK over there?" asked Julie.

The two got up in a dazed state and both replied, "Yeah, we're good."

"OK, I'm coming over," said Julie.

Julie walked, and putting one foot in front of the other, she tried not to fall off as the gate slowly swayed to and fro. She finally made it across the gate. "Let's never do that again."

"All right, come on," said Bryan quietly.

The group went straight and then took a right on the rooftops. "Shush," said Bryan. "We're on top of the residence of the pope."

"How do you know that?" asked Julie.

"Because we're—you know what? Never mind. Just be quiet; we don't want to awaken the guards," said Bryan.

"Well, sorry," said Julie in a sarcastic voice. The group tiptoed across the tile-studded rooftop and took a left turn.

Tyler looked down and saw the Courtyard of Saint Damaso and whispered to Bryan, "Bryan, look, there's a courtyard; we could go in through there."

"No. There are, like, a trillion doors in the museum, and there are tons and tons of keys; it would take forever to find the right key to open the door to the Hall of Tapestries. Let's just stick to our original plan," said Bryan.

"All right, fine, but next time we break into a building, I want to do it my way," said Tyler.

"Fine," replied Bryan.

"Would you guys stop debating whose plan is better and just do something?" said Julie. "OK, go straight and around this curved roof, and you will see a tower; we will go over or around the tower, whichever's easiest, and go out on the other side. Got it?" asked Bryan.

"Fine," exclaimed Tyler.

The group walked around the curved roof and slowly and carefully made their way to the tower trying not to drop the fake tapestry or the welding equipment. They successfully made it around the tower and slowly climbed down to the left side of the building and onto its slanted roof. The group trudged through the clay-tiled roofing to where they thought the Hall of Tapestries was. Bryan pulled out his blueprints from his back pocket with one hand while still holding the false tapestry in the other. "OK, just a few more feet."

The group walked a few more feet, and then Bryan signaled for the circular saw. He put his hand out for the saw, but then Julie put on the welding goggles and started cutting into the clay tiles in a large circle. Julie had to cut the tile on one side of the roof due to the roof's slant.

Finally, after two or three minutes, there was a circular hole that was about one yard in diameter. The debris from the roof hole fell straight down on the beautiful marble floor below. Bryan saw that there was a wooden crossbeam close to where Julie drilled the hole in the celling, Bryan grabbed the electric winch and attached the winch base to the wooden beam and once again connected his carabiner to the metal cable above the big black hook.

"OK, it's drilled," said Julie.

"Great. Now all we've got to do is go down, plug the keyholes in the doors at each end of the hallway, swap the tapestries, and get out by drilling a hole in the floor without getting caught," said Tyler.

"That's the plan," said Bryan.

Julie and Tyler connected their carabiners to the steel cable, right above Bryan's carabiner, and Julie pressed a button on the side of the electric winch; the three thieves were slowly lowered down to the ground floor. With the tapestry replica in Bryan's arms and the saw equipment attached to the hook, the group descended deeper and deeper into the darkness. Tyler pulled out a small flashlight from his pocket and turned it on. In the small circular light, they could see glimpses of fine pieces of art hanging on the walls. The group unclipped their carabiners from the cable so they could move around more freely.

Bryan ran down on one side of the hall to plug the doors with the hardening putty Gwardo had given him. "This is the Hall of Tapestries, all right," said Tyler.

Bryan then ran to the other side of the hall to plug the other doors. Julie pulled out her flashlight and peered around the long hall.

"OK, the tapestries are arranged in the order of Jesus's life, so let's spread out and find the Resurrection," said Bryan, panting after running to plug the keyholes.

The group spread out in different directions, trying to find the tapestry they were searching for. "Look, guys, over here!" Julie exclaimed. "I found it."

Bryan and Tyler rushed over to Julie. The tapestry was the fourth tapestry down the hall on the left side. The three turned and looked up at it. "How are we supposed to get that down off the hooks?" asked Tyler.

"I don't know," said Bryan.

"What, you don't know!" exclaimed Julie.

"Well, it looks like the tapestries are held by three short chains that are bolted onto the ceiling, and there is a steel rod connected to the chains," said Bryan.

Tyler went under the white rope barricade in front of the tapestry. He then looked around and shined his flashlight up toward the steel rod holding the tapestry. "Guys, we have a big problem," he declared.

"What?" asked Bryan.

"You know that steel metal rod that is holding the tapestry up?"

"Yeah, what about it?" asked Bryan.

"Well, connected to the rod is a pressure sensor. If we take the tapestry down, we will set off the alarm," said Tyler.

"Damn!" said Bryan.

The group was stumped as to how to remove the tapestry without setting off the alarm.

"Wait, what if we place the fake tapestry behind the real one and then attach the fake one to the rod and pull the real tapestry off?" said Julie.

"Oh, so like in the Indiana Jones movie, where he switched a sandbag for a golden idol?" said Tyler.

"I have no idea what you're talking about; I've never seen that movie," said Julie.

"So you've never seen *Indiana Jones*?"

"No; what's the big deal?" asked Julie.

"What's the big deal? Julie, *Indiana Jones* is one of the most brilliant movies in history," said Tyler.

"True. He's right," replied Bryan.

"And that's supposed to mean something?" asked Julie. "What, am I automatically supposed to know simply because you guys know?" said Julie.

"Well, not necessarily," said Tyler.

"I don't think that my boyfriend and his friend need to tell me what I should be watching because I decide who I am and what I do; you both should be ashamed of yourselves," exclaimed Julie.

Both guys put their heads down and rubbed their necks awkwardly, trying to avoid eye contact because they felt ashamed when they realized what they had done.

"Now that we've got that out of our systems, let's focus on the problem at hand, getting the tapestry," said Julie.

"I like your switching idea, but the only problem is, how are we going to get up there to place the fake tapestry behind the real one?" asked Bryan. "Could we use the winch?"

"What do you mean?" asked Tyler.

"Well, what if we use the winch to lift up the real tapestry by the bottom end, and then we stand on our shoulders and place the fake tapestry on the center bracket on the steel rod and then do that again for both of the other sides of the fake tapestry? Then we can pull the real one off that way so the weight sensor is not set off," said Bryan.

"I like that idea," said Tyler.

"OK, let's do it, then," said Julie.

With all three carrying the large tapestry on their shoulders single file, they placed it rolled up in front of the real tapestry. The group then lifted the real tapestry over the white rope boundary line as Tyler ran to the hanging silver cable from the winch and released the cable as far as it would go, then brought the cable to the tapestry. Bryan attached the bottom of the tapestry to the cable via another metal rod the tapestry. Tyler pressed a button on a small black remote in his hand that controlled the wench wirelessly, and the winch slowly raised the real tapestry up in the air. "Give the cable slack so we don't rip the tapestry," offered Bryan. The tapestry was now in the air hanging at an angle above them.

The group quickly got to work unwrapping the tapestry from its plastic tube, then went behind the white rope barrier and carried the fake tapestry over the barrier. One at a time, they stood on each other's shoulders—first

Tyler, second Bryan. Julie grabbed the end of the fake tapestry and handed it to Tyler to pass to Bryan. Once it was fully extended, Tyler passed the end of the fake tapestry to Bryan and then slowly but surely to Julie. Bryan reached with all his strength and placed the tapestry on the back of the metal rod. On the metal rod, there were two long metal slots on each side—one side was holding the real tapestry in place; the other slot, on the back end, was empty. Julie carefully slid one end of the tapestry into the less-than-one-inch-tall slot and then the other side. "Would you stop moving down there!" exclaimed Bryan.

"Sorry if I'm disturbing you, but you're also not trying to carry you on your shoulders," Tyler replied sarcastically.

While Tyler was talking, Bryan slid the other end into the slot. "Got it."

Tyler put Bryan down, breathing heavily.

"All right, now we have to remove the real tapestry from the metal rod," Bryan said.

"And turn the rod so it isn't showing," added Julie.

"Right," replied Tyler.

Then Tyler and Bryan once again stood on each other's shoulders, and Tyler slowly unclipped the tapestry from its holding slot on the rod. Because the other end of the tapestry was connected to the winch, the tapestry swung past them and like a pendulum stopped after it had gone back and forth a few times in the air. Meanwhile Bryan turned the rod slot forward, facing the hall, all the while keeping pressure on the sensor. Bryan then climbed back down again off Tyler's shoulders and was back on the marble flooring where they had started.

"Let's never do this again," offered Tyler. Bryan agreed, and Julie just stood there trying to hold in her laughter.

"What are you laughing about?" asked Bryan.

"You guys are so funny sometimes," exclaimed Julie.

Tyler used his black remote to control the winch and slowly lowered the real tapestry to the ground. Once the tapestry was on the ground, the lower rod was disconnected from the cable, and the tapestry lay flat on the ground. Suddenly an alarm rang out from every which way. "What just happened?" yelled Tyler.

"Yeah, what happened? We put it back right," said Julie.

"The fake tapestry must have been lighter than the real thing, and that must have triggered the sensor—hence the emergency alarm," yelled Bryan.

"Do you think they'll notice?" squealed Julie.

"Probably not. Gwardo has people who make custom, highly detailed work, and it's probably as close to the real thing as you can get," said Bryan.

"Who cares at this point? The alarms are going. What now?" yelled Tyler.

"You need to go get the welding equipment and cut through...hold on...which one is it? Um, oh, right there." Bryan pointed at a large square marble floor piece.

"Why are we cutting through the floor? The alarm went off," questioned Tyler with animation since the alarm was still ringing.

"Because under the floor, there are catacombs that lead all around Rome and the rest of Italy; we're going to use them as our escape tunnel."

"Awesome!" replied Tyler. He ran and got the circular saw and started to cut a hole in the floor. Meanwhile Julie and Bryan rolled up the real tapestry and placed it in the same plastic tube covering that they had used for the fake tapestry.

Tyler used the saw and the Dexpan and sliced though the floor like a hot knife through butter, and the floor tiles fell into the catacombs; finally a tunnel was visible. The group left the cutting equipment and the winch behind, dropped through the floor with the tapestry, and began to run though the underground maze like mice looking for cheese.

Meanwhile, above ground, the Vatican police were trying to bust in the doors, but the putty clogged the keyhole and delayed the police for around twenty minutes until they busted though the door using a handheld battering ram.

The police stumbled in and were trying to figure out what had set the alarm off. As Bryan had predicted, they didn't see anything missing; all they found were holes in the ceiling and the floor. Detective Mucillini of the Vatican police force was trying to put the whole puzzle together. "I want you to flood the catacombs!" said Detective Mucillini to one of his officers. The officer did as he was told, and the men brought in massive white hoses to pump the water into the catacombs.

Meanwhile, in the catacombs, Bryan, Julie, and Tyler were running for their lives, and after about half a mile or so, they decided to walk. "Man, I'm exhausted," declared Bryan.

"Yeah, me too," said Julie.

"Me three," replied Tyler, "and this tapestry isn't getting any lighter."

"Wait. Do you guys hear something?" asked Bryan.

"Hear what? I don't hear anything," replied Tyler.

Bryan then turned around and saw a large gush of water about nine meters behind him. "Go! Go! Run!"

"What? Why?" asked Julie. Then Julie looked behind her and saw the rushing water. "Oh crap."

All three ran as fast as they could with the tapestry on their shoulders. "I see light," yelled Bryan to the other two. The group ran toward the light, and they then saw beautiful green grass and bright sunlight. It seemed like the water behind them was subsiding.

"Man, what the heck happened?" asked Bryan.

"I don't know, but I'm so glad we're alive," said Tyler. The group celebrated with hugs and pats on the back, each one telling the others just how awesome they were. Gwardo's van drove up, and Gwardo had plastered a new sign, reading Oriental Carpets and Antiques, on the side. He got out of the driver's side of the van and helped the twenty-year-olds load the real tapestry into the van.

"Thanks, Gwardo," said Bryan.

"It's what I do," replied Gwardo.

He drove the van to the airport, where Bryan, Tyler, and Julie would fly back to DC. Then he drove to a FedEx center, put on a FedEx uniform, disguising himself as an employee, and cleared the tapestry through customs; it was off to DC.

The tired and exhausted group boarded the plane, knowing the tapestry was in their possession.

CHAPTER 5

TAPESTRY THEORIES

The plane landed in DC, and they went to customs, where a nice older lady working at the desk said, "Welcome back to the US." Bryan just fake smiled, trying to avoid a conversation with the older lady. Bryan, Tyler, and Julie grabbed their bags from the luggage area and went back to Bryan's house to study the tapestry more closely.

The group arrived back at Bryan's house, where they saw the tapestry waiting for them at their front door, along with a FedEx driver. "Is this your house, sir?" asked the driver.

"Yes, sir, it is," replied Bryan.

"Did you order this?" asked the driver.

"Yes, I did; it's a rug from Italy," replied Bryan.

"Will you please sign for it, then?" asked the driver. Bryan signed the paper.

Julie dropped her bags on the floor, exhausted. "I'm so glad were safe at home."

"Me too," replied Bryan, half yawning.

"Did you not sleep on the plane?" asked Tyler.

"No, I did; it's just been a long week," said Bryan.

"Tell me about it; I'm done," said Julie.

"Well, on that note, let's all take a nap and reconvene in an hour," said Bryan.

Bryan slept on the couch in the living room and Tyler and Julie in Bryan's bed. After about an hour of sleep, they reconvened in the living room, and Bryan brought in some store-bought sandwiches and coffee. The friends ate their snack while discussing the tapestry and decided to lay it out across the room.

After eating, they moved all the furniture from the living room and the rug under it to the kitchen. After they had removed everything and vacuumed the floor so the tapestry wouldn't get dirty, they laid it down on the wood floor.

It barely fit the space; there was only a small amount of space for them to walk around it. "There, it's in," said Tyler after unrolling the last of the tapestry.

"Now what does it mean?" asked Bryan.

"Well, the lady at the museum said it was connected to the ark of the covenant because that was supposedly the last place where it was stored and that's where Jesus walked after his resurrection," said Julie.

"Is the Resurrection even real? I mean, it could have just been a big hoax," said Tyler.

"I mean, I believe it's real," replied Bryan.

"Yeah, well, I believe that Jesus was a big fat liar," said Julie.

"All right, beliefs aside, what does this tapestry tell us?" asked Bryan.

The group looked at the tapestry with desperate eyes, scanning it for any clues. "Wait, so let's just backtrack for a minute and reconnect what we already know," said Julie. "OK, so Bryan found a copy of the Declaration of Independence."

"I was held at gunpoint, don't forget," replied Bryan in a stressed tone.

"Yeah, yeah. Anyway, then we decoded the message from the document, and that led us to the conclusion that the Freemasons were kicked out because the Catholic Church wanted to keep its power and because of the Freemasons' so-called dullness toward the church, and the Freemasons left England with the settlers on the *Mayflower* to continue their ways," said Julie. "Then we flew to the Vatican Archives and looked for the reasons they kicked the Freemasons out, and then we found the list of numbers leading us to the Masonic temple in Washington, DC," said Tyler.

"Then we went into the temple and went to the library and found the book that had the sentences 'It being seventy-seven hundred feet on a compass' and 'Trust the tapestry; the resurrection is near,'" said Bryan.

"We then we broke down the sentences and couldn't find out what the first one meant, so we went to the second one, and then, Bryan, you realized that we had to go back to the Vatican to go look at the tapestry that we now have in our possession," said Tyler.

"Then we had to steal the tapestry and replace it with a fake one so the Vatican authorities wouldn't notice, and surprisingly it worked," said Julie.

"And now here we are in your house looking at the tapestry that we illegally stole," said Tyler.

"You mean we *stole* it," said Bryan.

"What do you mean?" asked Tyler.

"Well, you said we *illegally* stole it," said Bryan.

"And that's what we did," replied Tyler.

"Well, we *stole* it. You can't legally steal something; therefore, stealing anything is illegal."

"Yeah, yeah, whatever. And your point is?"

"Nothing. I was just fixing your grammar."

"God, you're annoying."

"Me? What about you?" said Bryan. The boys started an argument, and Julie jumped in to keep them on track.

"Hey, guys, shut up," said Julie.

"What?" replied Bryan with a chuckle.

"Yeah, what were we doing?" asked Tyler.

"OMG. You guys are a mess; I'm not even going to answer that," replied Julie. "Can we please just focus and not argue?" The two guys nodded their heads in compliance.

"Thank you. Now what does this tapestry mean?" asked Julie.

"Maybe the Freemasons are hiding a symbol of some sort in the tapestry—remember that they like hiding things in symbols," said Bryan.

"Yeah, but what?" asked Tyler. The group looked at the tapestry very intensely.

"Wait, that guard in front, closer to Jesus, looking away," said Julie.

"What about him?" asked Bryan.

"No, not him, *her*," replied Julie.

"What? What do you mean?" asked Bryan.

"Well, he looks like a she, and she looks like she isn't afraid of Jesus but is turned away, and her eyes are looking at the ground like she knows something but doesn't want to express it through her face in fear that she would give something away," said Julie.

"Now how would you know that expression?" asked Bryan.

"Just simple facial cues," replied Julie.

"All right, then, if she is in fact a women, then who is she?" asked Tyler.

"She could be one of the women from one of the four Gospels who went to go see Jesus's body and make it smell nice as the body had decayed," said Bryan.

"Look at the man on the right side with the shield over his head," said Tyler.

"Yeah, and he's holding a metal shield over his head. Whoa, what?" asked Julie.

"Look at his face; he looks shocked, like the person who went into the grave came out a different person," said Tyler.

"Why is that?" asked Julie.

"Wait, can we please just address something first?" said Bryan.

"What?" asked Julie.

"Can we please just address that Jesus wasn't white?" said Bryan.

"Wait, he wasn't?" asked Julie.

"No, he wasn't. He was born in Nazareth, so his ethnicity was not white, and he was Jewish, so he had a light and dark tone," said Bryan.

"That's not true," said Julie.

"Well, we may not have a picture of Jesus, but we can see what modern Galileans and Middle Eastern Jews look like today for a possible reference," said Bryan.

"Well, than why is Jesus always depicted as white?" asked Tyler.

"Well, the Western culture wanted to make Jesus look like them because the Western culture, as I said before, like America, tried to shape the church and the views on Jesus to what they wanted," said Bryan. "And I'm not saying the way people in America preach Christianity or the Bible is wrong, because that would be wrong—I believe the Bible is true wherever you put it because it is the Word of God. But I think our perception of a white Jesus is wrong, and I think we need to be more open to different ethnicities in the church," said Bryan.

"Oh, that explains it," said Julie.

"OK, so back to the tapestry," said Tyler.

"Right, the tapestry, so the lady and the man wearing Roman armor have certain facial expressions, and that means what exactly?" asked Bryan.

"I think that the lady's expression means that she is hiding something about Jesus's resurrection, and looking at the man's expression—the way he is looking at Jesus when he walks out of the tomb probably means that he is either shocked that he has arisen from the dead or that the person who walked out of the tomb was a different person or both," replied Julie.

"So let's go with your theory: If this lady in Roman armor helped Jesus either regain his health or replaced him entirely, then who is she, and why is she helping him?" asked Tyler.

"Wait, say that again," said Julie.

"I said that whether the lady helped Jesus regain his health or replaced him entirely, we still don't know who she is," said Tyler.

"That's it—Jesus was replaced," said Julie.

"No, no, that can't be true because that would mean that there would have to be two Jesuses, and that would ruin the whole main belief of Christianity," said Bryan.

"That must be the secret that the Freemasons were hiding," said Julie.

"You're probably right," said Tyler.

"I can't believe you guys; you can't actually believe that there were two Jesuses," said Bryan.

"Well, actually, it does seem quite plausible," said Julie.

"How so?" asked Bryan.

"Well, if there were two Jesuses, then let's say one lived and died on the cross, and then they brought him to the tomb and rolled over the stone; then someone snuck into the tomb, like the three women who went into the tomb to make the dead body smell good, like it says in the Gospels, but one of them wasn't a woman and was a Jesus look-alike. And then the two women walked out, and the guard rolled back the tombstone, and the man took Jesus's body out of the burial cloth, burnt his body, then pierced his own hands and feet with a nail he had brought with him. The man put on Jesus's clothes, burnt his own clothes, and then went and folded the burial cloth," said Julie.

"OK, but how the man would get out of the tomb?" asked Bryan.

"He must have pushed the stone from the inside and then left it open and masqueraded as Christ. That's why when the disciples see him for the first time after the Resurrection, they don't believe it's him, and then Jesus shows them the holes in his hands and feet, and they believe him because there is evidence," said Tyler.

"I can't believe that; I'm sorry, but I just can't," replied Bryan.

"Bryan, I'm sorry, but that's the truth," said Julie.

"No, see, that's a theory; that's not true. I won't believe it," said Bryan.

"All right, believe what you want, but I know truth when I see it," said Tyler.

"Truth? That's not truth; that's absolute heresy," proclaimed Bryan.

Tyler and Bryan's heated argument continued for a few more moments, then suddenly, out of nowhere, Bryan's front door got blown off its hinges. The CIA and a SWAT team marched in carrying heavy automatic weapons, and within the blink of an eye, the three college students got thrown to the hard wooden floor, and things became very blurry as Bryan instantly lost consciousness.

CHAPTER 6

MISDIRECTION

B ryan woke up in a military helicopter hundreds of feet up in the air. Julie and Tyler woke up moments after Bryan. The group was sitting on netted seats side by side, and two military personnel were at the opposite side of the chopper. Bryan started to get up but realized that he couldn't because he was in cuffs and was strapped down. "Morning, lady and gentlemen," said the officer.

"What is this? Why are we here!" demanded Julie.

"All your questions will be answered soon enough," replied the officer. Julie sat back again and tried to relax amid the extremely tense situation.

The helicopter flew for a few more minutes, and the group remained silent as the rotary blades spun outside above their heads. "Welcome to Langley, Virginia," said the officer.

The three captives looked out the window and saw a large glass-covered building. "Wait, we're going to CIA headquarters?" asked Bryan.

"Yes, sir," replied the officer.

The helicopter hovered over a helipad on the grounds of the headquarters; as soon as the chopper landed, the three students got yanked out of the netted seat, and with their heads ducked, trying not to hit the spinning blades above them, they got out and were escorted by the officers to the front of the building, all three still cuffed.

The front doors of the building opened, and they saw a woman in her midforties in a white pantsuit and two CIA agents standing at either side of her.

"Hello, Bryan," said the mysterious figure in the pantsuit.

"How do you know my name?" asked Bryan forcefully.

"We know a lot about you, Bryan, because we're the CIA. Now come with me," said the lady in the suit.

The CIA agents on the left and right of her guided them through the doors while the military officers saluted, turned, and went back to their helicopter and their previous posts. Bryan, Tyler, and Julie were led though the large glass front doors and down the white halls of the building.

"So why are we here, and who are you exactly? Because I still don't know, and it's kind of freaking me out," exclaimed Tyler.

"You will know soon enough," said the woman. She then opened a large glass door and the group went in; she shut the door, and it door locked automatically once it closed. In the center of the room was a large metal table and four metal chairs, three on one side of the table and one on the other side. There were also four tan file cabinets on the back wall. "Please sit," said the woman.

The three students sat down on the side with three chairs, and the woman sat on the other side. "Now you are probably wondering who I am," said the woman.

"Thank God. Finally," said Tyler.

"Don't use God's name in vain," replied Bryan.

"Oh, really? Well, I'm sorry for insulting you, then!" said Tyler in a snarky tone.

"Gentlemen, gentlemen!" said the woman.

"What!" they both said spontaneously together.

"We are here to discuss national security, not your religious differences," said the woman. "Now you're probably wondering who I am."

"Uh, yeah," replied Julie in a sassy tone.

"Well, my name is Mrs. Burns. I am the director of the CIA. As such I am prepared to deal with all types of threats, national and otherwise," said the director.

"And are we a threat?" asked Julie.

"That remains to be seen," replied the director. The director got up out of her chair and went and opened one of the tan file cabinets and pulled out a few files. She shut the file cabinet and returned to her seat and placed the stack of three files on the cold metal table. She then placed a file in front of each young person and opened it for them since they were cuffed. In each file there was a picture of the subject and dozens of pages of blacked-out information.

"Wait, that's my picture and my information. Who gave you the authority to take this!" demanded Bryan.

"We're the CIA. We can do anything we need to do to analyze threats when—and hopefully before—they take shape," said the director. The three prisoners looked at their picture and then the information that was not covered over in black Sharpie.

"Why do you have files on us?" asked Julie.

"Yeah, we're not threats; we're just normal," said Tyler.

"We need to be prepared for any and all situations; it's just protocol," replied the director.

"So where are you from, Director? If you know all about us, why can't we know a little bit about you?" asked Tyler.

"Very well. If you truly must know, I was raised on military bases. My dad was a general officer in the army; we moved around a lot. I never truly got to make very many friends, and that's probably why I ended up in the intelligence community, because that's basically all I knew."

"What about your mom?" asked Julie in a sincere tone.

"She passed away a number of years ago. Anyway, that's not important, and I would prefer not to discuss it; what's important right now is doing my job. Now on to the real issue at hand." The director closed the files and stacked them on top of one another, placing them on one side of the table and then sniffling. The director then grabbed the last file on the other side of her and placed it in the center of the table. "This is why you were brought here." She opened the file.

"That's the guy who held me at gunpoint and who we saw at the Freemason temple," said Bryan.

"His name is Luis Ivanov; he was a Russian spy and was sent by the Russian government to find a mysterious religious object with ultimate power," said the director.

"How did you find us?" asked Julie.

"When you stole the tapestry, we looked at all the air traffic in the area and the general time of day when it was supposedly stolen and traced all the packages and the size as well as the shape, among other things," said the director.

"Oh, that explains a lot," said Bryan.

"What I want to know is what he is after and whether we can get it first. Then we can use that as leverage to bring Ivanov in and bring him to a trial and later justice. So will you help us bring him down?" asked the director.

"All right, we'll help you," said Bryan.

"What? Hold on a minute," said Julie.

"Yeah, hold on a minute, lady. Let me get this straight—you have a SWAT team break into my friend's house—which is pretty awesome, ain't gonna lie—but anyway, you kidnap us and bring us here against our will and ask us to help you bring in a Russian lunatic that was sent to find some artifact that could somehow lead to our demise!" said Tyler.

"So who's in?" asked the director.

"Hell ya. I'm in!" replied Tyler.

"What? Guys, are you insane?" asked Julie.

"What? No," said Bryan.

"Yeah, we're smart; I've got a brain on me," replied Tyler cockily.

"If they're both in, I have to be in too," responded Bryan.

"Fine, I'm in too," said Julie. "Now can we please take these hand cuffs off?"

The director got the key out of her front jacket pocket and unlocked the three handcuffs.

Finally, with their hands free, rubbing their wrists and shoulders from the uncomfortable binding, they got to work.

"So let's go over what we already know," said Bryan.

"Well, we know that Ivanov is going after the artifact that we are going after; that's why we saw him outside in the hall of the library of the Freemason temple," said Tyler.

"Right, and in the library, we found two phrases, one leading to the tapestry and one that we still can't figure out, about something being seventy-seven hundred feet on a compass," said Bryan.

"As you already know, we kinda stole the resurrection of Jesus tapestry from the Vatican Museum," said Julie.

"You could have caused an international incident if you haven't already," said the director.

"But don't worry—we replaced it with a replica," said Tyler.

"Oh my God," said the director as she paced back and forth in distress.

"Anyway, then we figured out a bunch of theories and symbols in the tapestry," said Julie.

"Now we just need to figure out what the measurement means," replied Bryan.

"It sounds like a map or a location," replied the director.

"Why would you say that?" asked Bryan.

"If I remember my history right, surveyors used compasses to measure land distances," said the director.

"Wait, George Washington was a surveyor and a Freemason," said Bryan.

"How did you connect that so quickly?" asked the director.

"Well, I was a giving a presentation on the Freemasons at the college I go to, and something just clicked, before I was cut off," said Bryan.

"What do you mean?" asked the director.

"I ran out of time because the person who went before me took too much of my time, and now it is one and a half weeks late because I am entangled in this mess," replied Bryan.

"Looks like we need a map," said Tyler.

"Of what, though?" asked Julie.

"Well, George Washington surveyed the land for his biggest estate," said Bryan.

"Wait, you don't mean?" asked Julie.

"Exactly…Washington, DC," said Bryan.

The CIA director asked for a map of the DC area and rolled it out on the metal table. "OK, so the surveyors always started at the origin, or point zero point zero," said Bryan. "But we need the origin from the year in which it was being built, which was 1790."

The director googled the point of origin for Washington, DC. "The origin was the Capitol building," she said.

Bryan circled the Capitol on the map and placed the word "origin" above it. He then saw a subtle sign on the map and started to draw. "What are you doing?" asked the director.

Bryan drew a line down Pennsylvania Avenue and a line down Maryland Avenue from the Capitol building all the way down to Pennsylvania South and the equivalent distance on the other side. "Wait, that looks like a compass," replied Julie. "And if we draw a line from Eleventh Street across to the World War II Memorial and from the World War II Memorial diagonally to the Washington Channel, we get the Freemason logo of a compass and the square."

"Well, I'll be dammed," said the director.

"It being seventy-seven hundred feet on a compass," said Julie.

"OK, so we found the compass, but what exactly is it?" said Tyler.

"It would have to be connected to the Freemasons or George Washington because George Washington built Washington, DC," said Julie.

"Wait, that's it. In the seventeen nineties, there were cornerstones built under each remaining monument, but the one in the Capitol has never been found, and the one that has never been found was personally placed by George Washington, who was a Freemason," said Bryan.

"But where was the cornerstone placed?" asked Julie.

"It must have been placed at the seventy-seven-hun-dred-foot point in the compass," said Bryan.

"But which direction?" asked Tyler.

"I don't know," replied Bryan.

"But what if we miss a direction?" asked the director.

"Let's just pray that we pick the right one; let's try the center first," said Bryan.

"That must be it; I will get a team together, and we'll move out immediately!" said the director.

CHAPTER 7

THE CORNERSTONE

The director led Bryan, Julie, and Tyler out a side door and to a gray van in the parking lot. The director opened the sliding door of the van, and the group got in along with two CIA agents. "OK, we've got a twenty-five-minute drive, so buckle up, and let's go find this cornerstone," said the director. The gray van was accompanied by two black Cadillac Escalades, one behind and one in front. The group headed out of the secure location of the CIA headquarters and into the vicinity of the Capitol building.

"So what are we looking for exactly on the cornerstone?" asked the director.

"Well, we could be looking for an inscription on the top of the stone or an engraving of some sort," replied Bryan.

"So once we have the cornerstone, then what?" asked Tyler.

"We probably will need to connect the cornerstone and the tapestry somehow, and that will lead us to the powerful item Luis Ivanov was after in the first place," replied Bryan.

"I was looking at the location on the map, and I will need to call for backup and get the FBI involved because the CIA can't technically operate on US soil," said the director. She called the FBI director and eventually got his approval.

"How long do we have to wait until the FBI shows up?" asked Julie.

"The FBI is setting up a perimeter as we speak," replied the director.

"Great—now we have space to work," said Julie. Julie grabbed Tyler's hand in a tight embrace.

*　*　*

The van door slid open, and the group got out and was met with a long stretch of bright-yellow caution tape. Bryan surveyed the scene and saw about fifty FBI agents in blue-and-yellow jackets scanning the ground with lasers and digging it up with shovels. "They're looking in the wrong place," he said.

"What do you mean?" asked the director.

Bryan pointed at the map. "Right now, we're digging at the base of the Capitol building, but we're supposed to be digging seventy-seven hundred feet from here," said Bryan.

The CIA director spoke with the FBI director and told him the news. "All right, we've got new orders to dig seventy-seven hundred feet from here!" said the FBI director into his earpiece microphone.

One of the FBI agents got into his car and led the rest with a digital measuring device; he drove down the street, passing the reflecting pool and the American Indian Museum, then stopped at the Air and Space Museum. The FBI director got out of his car and walked up to the agent; he leaned out his window and then yelled, "All right, mount up!" Almost immediately a perimeter of yellow tape was set up and a grid established within the cordoned-off zone.

Bryan stood with Julie and Tyler on the sidelines and watched as the small army dug fast and swiftly through the dirt. After around ten minutes, one of the agents signaled the FBI director that they had found something. The FBI agents unpegged the string grid and moved it to the side.

The agents dug around the object, and then a small group lifted the object out of the ground. Two agents carried the object to a metal table set up off to the side and began dusting it off with brushes. The two directors and the three students ran to the table to view the object. The object was a rectangular rusty metal tin about one foot by two feet by about one and a half feet in height.

The FBI agent opened the rusty box, and in it was a letter encased in between two thin pieces of glass so it wouldn't degrade. The agent gave it to the FBI director, who read it aloud. "'I shall give thee what thou want if thee think backward and retrace thou steps. To thou Ideologies shall ones possess shall pass. Therefore, go northwest, and ye turn ye back on where ye think to find what one possess.'

"Does this mean anything to you?" asked the FBI director.

"Here, let me see that," said Bryan. The FBI director handed the letter to Bryan. Bryan read the letter over again and saw a wax seal with the Freemason symbol of the all-seeing eye on it, at the bottom left corner. "Retracing our steps—so we probably have to go back to the Capitol building," said Bryan.

Once they had returned to the Capitol building, Julie asked, "OK, what does the rest of the letter mean?"

"Well, the letter mentions ideologies, and the Freemasons' ideologies are pretty deep," replied Bryan.

"What do you mean?" asked Tyler.

"Well, the Freemasons believed in the brotherhood and making better men and being closer to God," said Bryan.

"So one had to possess those values to enter the place where the cornerstone was hidden?" asked Julie.

"Well, you believe in God, so you'll be good, then," said Tyler.

"Right," replied Bryan sarcastically.

"Then it says to go southwest," said the CIA director.

"Right," said Bryan.

The group walked around to the northwest side of the Capitol building. "OK, now what?" asked the FBI director.

"Well, the letter says to turn your back on where you think it is," said Bryan.

The group turned their backs on the northwest side of the building, and Bryan realized the answer to the riddle. "The letter is telling us to go to the southeast corner."

"But why? We're facing the right way," said Tyler.

"No, we're not. See—the letter says if you turn your back you will find what you possess, a.k.a. your back is leading the way, which means we would be facing the southeast corner. The cornerstone must be in the southeast corner," declared Bryan.

"Of course, in 1991 the government ordered a search for the Capitol cornerstone, but it was never found, and they thought it was in the opposite side," said the FBI director.

"What's under the southeast side?" asked Tyler.

"The National Statuary Hall," said the CIA director.

The group entered the Capitol building after the two directors showed their badges to security. They were followed by a few operatives. The group went down a long hallway and was led into the National Statuary Hall.

The hall itself was large and had a black-and-white-tiled floor and white marble and bronze statues of important historical figures. There were tall marble columns and a large golden chandelier in the center. "Where do we go now?" asked Julie. Bryan looked at the tile on the floor.

"I need a power drill!" demanded Bryan. The FBI director looked at the CIA director, and then the latter called for the power drill on her walkie-talkie. It was brought by one of the agents to Bryan. Bryan kneeled down and began drilling in the center of the floor. "Whoa, whoa, whoa, you can't do that!" says the FBI director.

"Oh, really? Why can't he?" demanded Julie, getting in his face.

"Because he is destroying the floor of our forefathers," said the FBI director. Bryan drilled a small hole in the floor and put a finger in the hole; he pulled up the tile, revealing an open space between the floorboards. Tyler leaned over Bryan and shined a flashlight into the hole, and the group was in awe at what they found.

"The cornerstone," said Tyler.

"Here, help me lift it out," said Bryan. Tyler, Bryan, Julie, and both of the directors were in a circle around the hole. The group removed some of the surrounding tiles and got down into the ditch with the cornerstone. Using all of their strength, they passed it up to the agents above, and they all got out of the ditch and examined the gray eroded cornerstone.

"I can't believe it was here the whole time," said the CIA director.

The group looked at the stone with its rectangular shape and silver engraved front plate. "How did you know it was in the floor?" asked Tyler.

"Well, I thought back to the letter, and when it said, 'One's ideologies one must possess,'" I think it meant to think like a Freemason, and Freemasons think logically— so that's what I did," said Bryan.

Julie looked at the cornerstone and realized there were nails holding the inscribed plate onto the actual stone. "I need a hammer," said Julie.

"Why?" asked the CIA director.

"Don't ask why; just get it!" said Julie.

The CIA director called in for a hammer, and an agent walked in a few moments later with a hammer. The agent handed the hammer to Julie, and she began to remove the nails from the metal plate attached to the stone. After removing the rusty nails in each of the four corners, she took the rectangular metal plate off to reveal a hollow center.

The group bunched closer to one another, waiting impatiently for the reveal of an object or clue hidden inside. Julie pulled out a letter written and signed by George Washington himself, a green marble triangle with an engraving of the all-seeing eye, and a brown leather book with "In God We Trust" on it.

"All right, we need to keep these under wraps," said the CIA director. Just then a man pushing a yellow cleaning cart walked across the floor. The man began to grab a pistol from his cleaning cart and let off two shots; the group crouched down, and the man ran off.

"It's Ivanov!" said Bryan after getting a look at him.

One of the agents chased after Ivanov, and Bryan ran to catch up to the agent. Bryan was followed by Julie and then Tyler, all sprinting.

The group lost Ivanov and headed back to the National Statuary Hall. "We need to put you three into protective custody," said the CIA director.

"Why?" asked Bryan.

"Because you three are now bloody targets," replied the CIA director.

CHAPTER 8

THE SEVEN SEALS

The group was driven back to the CIA headquarters, and each one of the students was placed in a separate small room enclosed in glass. Julie was in the left room, Bryan was in the middle, and Tyler was on the right. They were still able to see one another through the transparent panels of glass. Each room had a metal table and two chairs with four legs; Bryan figured this was where they normally did interrogations.

The CIA director walked into Bryan's room and asked him, "What's our next move?"

Bryan replied, "Our next move? How are we supposed to move if we are in solitary confinement?"

"Number one, we're working together, and number two, this is not solitary confinement; it's where we do interrogations. And three, I'm trying to find a loophole so I can get you out of here," said the director.

"Well, if you wanted us out of here so badly, why did you put us in here!" exclaimed Bryan.

"It's just protocol; even government agencies have rules," replied the director.

"Can I borrow your wallet?" asked Bryan.

"Why?" asked the director.

"Do you want to know our next move or not?" asked Bryan. The director handed over the wallet while Julie and Tyler peered in at Bryan on either side of him through the glass walls. Bryan pulled out a one-dollar bill and flipped it over to the backside. "Now you see that there?" Bryan pointed to the left circle with a pyramid on it. "The pyramid in this picture is the all-seeing eye. Do you see these letters around it? Well, if you reconfigure the letters, it spells 'a new world order.'"

"And how does that help us?" asked the director.

"Well, it is believed that the Freemasons are connected to the creation of a new world order," replied Bryan.

"That's ridiculous," replied the director.

"The all-seeing eye could represent one singular government, like a monarchy and the caste system and bringing all world leaders together, through Freemasonry," said Bryan.

"There is no way that is even plausible," said the director.

"Well, it actually is because fourteen US presidents have been Freemasons; they could have been shifting and molding the country for the sole purpose of bringing forth the Antichrist, and he could very well be a Freemason," replied Bryan.

"OK, I'm still not following," said the director.

"See the words 'In God We Trust'? Well, if we put ourselves back in the time when this was created, then we can get the context, and the basic context is that the Freemasons believed in Christianity and believed that

God was at the center of everything. Using that context, we can see that they probably read the Bible and the book of Revelation, which is the last book of the Bible."

"OK, I understand—the Freemasons are trying to control the world by creating a singular world order. Now please continue," said the director.

"In Revelation there are supposedly seven seals. Bryan pulled out a hundred-dollar bill, a fifty, a twenty, a ten, a five, and one two-dollar bill from the director's wallet and lined them up in order next to the one-dollar bill on the table.

"Now, in Revelation there are seven seals, and there are seven forms of US paper currency. We've done the one-dollar bill, so now let's go to the two-dollar bill," said Bryan. "On the back of the two-dollar bill, there is a picture of John Trumbull's *Declaration of Independence*, a painting now held by Yale University," said Bryan.

The director pulled up a picture of the original painting because the currency picture was so faded. "OK, so I see George Washington, Benjamin Franklin, John Adams, John Handcock, and Thomas Jefferson," said the director.

"I see Robert R. Livingston and Roger Sherman," said Bryan.

"So what is this supposed to tell us?" asked the director.

"Well, it was the signing of the Declaration of Independence, and more than half of the men we mentioned were Freemasons, so maybe it's telling us that Freemasons built America and they were here from the start, manipulating our government," said Bryan.

"OK, let's go to the five-dollar bill now," said the director.

"OK, so the five-dollar bill has the Lincoln Memorial on it," said Bryan.

"It kind of looks like a Greek temple," said the director.

"Not necessarily. It has columns, twelve to be exact, but that doesn't necessarily make it a Greek design, and why twelve?" asked Bryan.

"Could it relate to something religious?" asked the director.

"Actually that's not a bad idea; would you please google why the number twelve is significant in Christianity?" said Bryan. The director typed that into her laptop.

"OK, here are some possible answers: you have the twelve tribes of Israel, the number twelve is a representation of authority and perfection, and it is a symbol of divine rule and the perfect government of God and a singular order," said the director.

"OK, so let's remove the twelve tribes because it doesn't make sense in this context, but the second one is perfect because it deals with God's rule and perfect government," said Bryan. "And let's just recap what we know. The theory is that the one-dollar bill it showed us that the Freemasons were creating a global world order, and the two-dollar bill showed us that the Freemasons were intertwined in our government and there from the creation of our country, and the five-dollar bill told us about God's so-called perfect government."

"Right. What does the ten-dollar bill tell us?" asked the director.

"Well, they changed the design of the ten-dollar bill in 2006; the 1862 version had two Xs on the back with an oval in the middle," said Bryan.

"How do you know that?" asked the director.

"When your dad's a banker and your mom's a historian, you grow up with history and a good eye for money," replied Bryan.

The director pulled up an image of the 1862 ten-dollar bill. "Could the two Xs mean tens, as in Roman numerals?" she asked.

"I think you might be right," said Bryan. "The number ten is significant to Christianity because of the Ten Commandments, so maybe the reference is to laws or the judicial system."

"OK. What about the twenty-dollar bill?" asked the director.

"Well, there were again multiple versions of the twenty-dollar bill, starting with the greenback from 1875, but we want the version from 1891 because it looks cooler, in my opinion."

"Then why did we use the ten-dollar bill from 1862?" asked the director.

"We needed one of the original banknotes because the Freemasons have been here since the American settlers came, so using currencies from different time periods doesn't necessarily matter. The Freemasons kept the messages the same throughout each version so they would know what to do to prepare for the Antichrist's rise to power," said Bryan. "The only reason we are focusing on the 1891 version is because it was the one issued in closest proximity to the time when George Washington was still in office, and since Washington was a Freemason and we have the items from within the cornerstone that Washington supposedly placed, I just thought it would be more relevant."

"OK, I have pulled up a picture of the 1891 version of the twenty-dollar bill," said the director.

The two examined the picture of the back of the twenty-dollar bill for any relevant iconography. "I don't see any religious references," said Bryan.

Julie and Tyler started tapping on the glass. "What?" exclaimed Bryan "Can you bring them in here please?"

"Fine, though this is against protocol!" said the director. She unlocked the doors to the other rooms, and Tyler and Julie joined them in Bryan's room. The four now set about breaking the code on the twenty-dollar bill.

"What if it's an anagram?" asked Julie.

"I don't know," replied Bryan.

"Well, to me it just looks like an oval," said Tyler.

"What did you just say?" asked Bryan.

"I just said it just looks like an oval," replied Tyler.

"You're right—because that's what it is," said Bryan.

"I'm not following," said the director.

"The oval—as in the Oval Office," said Bryan.

"Wait, you mean to tell me that the oval on this bill is a reference to the Oval Office?" asked Julie.

"Yes," said Bryan.

"But George Washington never lived in the White House," said the director.

"You're right, but he built it," replied Bryan. "I need the blueprints of the original White House before the add-ons and renovations."

The director pulled up the blueprints from the online Library of Congress database. The group peered at the blueprints in the computer screen. "Where's the Oval Office?" asked Bryan, confused.

"It says here that the Oval Office was only completed in 1909," said Julie.

"I guess it wasn't there at the time of Washington," said Tyler.

"OK, back to the drawing board. Let's use the modern twenty-dollar bill because it will probably be easier, and since the message on each bill doesn't change throughout time, as I said before; we should be fine," replied Bryan.

"I think that Bryan has had his fun solving his puzzle; now it's my turn. May I?" asked Julie.

"Be my guest," said Bryan.

Julie looked at the modern version of the twenty-dollar bill on the table. She flipped it over, and on the back was a picture of the White House. "OK, so you were right about the White House, but it might not be about the Oval Office," she said.

"So you will admit I was close?" asked Bryan.

"Sure, you were close," said Julie.

"Yes, *boom*, that's how we do it," said Bryan, raising his hand for a high five; he put his hand down after a few seconds because he had been left hanging.

"So, what is it about the White House?" asked Julie.

"It could be a way of talking about the system it upholds?" said Tyler.

"Or someone in it," said Julie.

"What do you mean?" asked Bryan.

"The president."

"Do you mean the person or the position?" asked the director.

"The position," said Julie.

"So do you think the Freemasons are controlling the presidency?" asked Tyler.

"I think so, because fourteen of our presidents have been Freemasons," said Bryan.

"And that some of our voting machines were hacked?" said Tyler.

"All right, let's not get into politics; let's just go on to the fifty-dollar bill," said the director. Tyler flipped the fifty-dollar bill over.

"It's the Capitol building," exclaimed the director.

"Exactly. When we went to the Capitol building to find the cornerstone, this image on the bill triggered my memory, and that's why we're decoding these images," said Bryan.

"So that's why you asked for my wallet?" asked the director.

"Yeah. Each one of the bills has an image on the back, and supposedly each image is one of the seven seals," replied Bryan.

"When you put them into context, you see the message the Freemasons are giving the supposed Antichrist when he rises from the human race to destroy humanity.

The Freemasons want to be spared, so they are preparing by giving a message down through the ages to mold our society into a sinful world in hopes to be spared by the Antichrist," said Julie.

"How do you know that?" asked the director.

"I read it in that book we found at the Masonic temple library," said Julie.

"What do we know about the fifty-dollar bill and the Capitol building?" asked Tyler.

"Well, there was a riot at the Capitol building, and people dressed as Republicans and broke in," said Bryan.

"Dressed as? I say they were Republicans, and all they wanted was for Trump to win," said Tyler.

"That is absolute heresy," said Bryan.

"Heresy? You want to talk about heresy? May I remind you about the whole tapestry ordeal we were in right before the SWAT team busted down your door!" replied Tyler.

"By the way, you guys need to go retrieve the tapestry," said Bryan.

"I will have one of my agents bring it here immediately," said the director.

"There is also a file on my desk in my room; will you get that as well?" asked Bryan.

"Yes," said the director.

"Thank you, and as I was saying, the tapestry does not contradict Jesus's resurrection because I believe that he did die and rose again on the third day, and that's just reality!" exclaimed Bryan.

"I'm not just going to sit here and take this!" replied Tyler.

Tyler swung his right fist into Bryan's jaw. "What the hell, man!" said Bryan with blood dripping down his face; he wiped it off with his hand and shoved Tyler against the wall. They began to twist and turn until they were down on the ground pounding one another like wild gorillas. Julie jumped in between them and held her hands out to push them back from each other.

"Guys, stop it, or I will strike you where it hurts!" said Julie. Tyler pushed Julie aside and began to fight again. Before Tyler could land one more punch, the director shot a gun up into the air, and they both froze in their tracks.

With ceiling tile dust floating down from where she had shot, the angered CIA director walked toward the two young men. Their eyes were full of glossy fear, and they shrank back from their boyish pursuits and let go of each other for a moment to face the wrath of the woman standing before them. "Gentlemen, you must be ashamed of yourselves!" said the director. The young men looked down and around, trying not to make eye contact with her. "You two are friends, and right now there are bigger things at stake than your petty squabbles; do you understand me?" she asked in a firm voice.

"Yes," Bryan replied, and a few moments later, Tyler did as well.

"Great. There is an image of the Capitol building on a dollar bill, and there is no explanation. Who has ideas?" asked the director.

"Well, we did just find the cornerstone there with the green marble triangular eye, the letter from George Washington, and the brown leather book," said Julie.

"See, now there is a wonderful idea," said the director.

"It could have something else to do with the Capitol, like controlling the legislative branch, much like the presidency," said Tyler.

"Great idea—took the words right out of my mouth," said Bryan sarcastically.

"All right, then on to the one-hundred-dollar bill," said the director.

Bryan flipped the bill over to reveal an image of Independence Hall. "That's where they signed the Declaration of Independence."

"Duh, of course it was," said Tyler.

"Independence Hall is synonymous with American independence itself," said Bryan.

"And that means what, exactly?" asked Tyler.

"Well, that means what the one-hundred-dollar bill is trying to tell us is that Independence Hall is where the document was signed, and the document stated that we wanted our independence," said Bryan.

"Wow, real philosophical," said Tyler sarcastically.

"All right, I'm still confused," said Julie.

"Basically it's saying that some of our founding fathers were Freemasons and as such secretly manipulated the society into fully breaking away from Great Britain and set up the country's independence so they could one day take it over," said Bryan.

"But how is that even possible?" asked the director.

"Well, as I said to you two before, the Freemasons came over from Great Britain on the *Mayflower*, but even before that, there were British Freemasonry lodges in England, so all they had to do was to come to America and manipulate it in such a way that they could eventually have complete power and control over the United States," said Bryan.

"So what you're saying—and what the seven seals slash seven US bills are saying—is that the Freemasons are creating a new world order from the beginning, forming the laws, controlling who the president is, and shaping the House and the Senate and the judicial branch to control the United States?" said Julie.

"Yeah, basically—that's one way to summarize it all," said Bryan.

"Holy crap!" declared the director. "How are they going to do it?"

"I don't know, but I'm going find out," declared Bryan.

CHAPTER 9

RELIGIOUS TOLERANCE

Bryan pulled the director aside. "Could we go see a pastor?" he asked.

"Why?" asked the director.

"Because it would help me think through all of this more deeply," said Bryan.

The director thought for a moment. "OK, but we will be no more than a block away." She was a little worried for his safety.

The group drove to the Immaculate Conception Church.

"Why this church?" asked Julie.

"Yeah, I thought you weren't Catholic," said Tyler.

"You're right, I'm not, but this was the church my parents used to take me to when I was younger," replied Bryan.

"You know, for all the years I've known you, I never once knew what you truly believed," said Tyler.

"Well, in high school I was struggling with a lot of things, and I was in and out of church a lot and never really summited myself in the faith," replied Bryan.

"Then why do you believe it now?" asked Julie.

"Well, I realized after a while that I needed Jesus because the truth is religion just wasn't going to cut it for me anymore," replied Bryan.

"But I thought Christianity was a religion?" asked Tyler.

"It is, but I realized that my faith wasn't really my faith; it was just me trying to follow laws and trying to be perfect," said Bryan.

"Who cares? It's your life," said Tyler.

"I do. I realized that I never needed to be perfect for Jesus to love me because as humans we're not perfect due to our sin and all the mistakes that we have made. Jesus covered our mistakes in his blood on the cross when he died," replied Bryan.

"Some God to let his son suffer like that," said Julie.

"Well, the story wasn't over. Jesus was lying in a tomb for three days and then rose again and walked the earth," replied Bryan.

"And that lady at the Vatican Museum said the ark of the covenant was placed where Jesus walked after the Resurrection for a while," said Julie.

"Exactly," exclaimed Bryan, realizing the connection between those two things in his head.

"What happened next?" asked Tyler.

"Well, he walked the earth a bit and then ascended into heaven," replied Bryan.

"So what are you saying exactly?" asked Tyler.

"OK, I'll summarize. Basically, I simply believe that Jesus is the son of God and that he died for our sins and mistakes and that there is a difference between people who say they are Christians and people who have a real relationship with him. When you are saved, you are saved once and for all, and you are saved not by your own works, like Catholicism says, but by grace through faith," said Bryan.

"What do you say to all the people who are Catholic and contradict that?" asked Julie.

"Well, I would just give them Titus 3:5: 'He saved us, not because of the righteous things we had done but because of his mercy,'" replied Bryan boldly.

"So you seriously think that Catholicism is wrong?" asked Tyler.

"I don't necessarily believe that it's wrong because all Christian denominations have problems and issues; we're all sinful human beings, and we're not perfect. The church isn't perfect, and the church isn't called to be perfect; it is called to show love and compassion to others and love Jesus. Just look at the early church, and the church today, even—the point is we're all broken, and we need Jesus, not religion, to fix us," replied Bryan.

The group arrived at the church, and Bryan got out of the black sedan, which drove off and parked a block away. Bryan walked up the concrete steps and entered the church. He looked around the vast room; it was just as he remembered it. Dark-brown floors and long rows of wooden pews filled the room, and there was a large white pulpit in the front with stained glass windows. Father Charles, the pastor of the church, was standing by one of the windows, looking out.

"Father?" said Bryan.

"Ah, Bryan, I was waiting for you," said Father Charles.

"How did you know I was coming?"

"I felt the Spirit move," said Father Charles. "That or I saw you from the window. What can I do for you, my son?"

Bryan sat on a wooden pew. "I have been having doubts about my faith, Father."

Father Charles then sat in the pew next to Bryan with a concerned look on his face.

"In what way?"

"I have been struggling in the way of whether Jesus really did die on the cross and whether religion or science is right—or if they fit together."

"As a priest I would say that religion is right and that he did, but I know you probably wanted a little bit of a different answer."

"Well, it's just so conflicting because there is so much evidence both ways."

"What type of evidence?"

"Well, for the Resurrection, there were eyewitnesses like Mother Mary, but it could all be a trick—what if she was in on it?"

"In on what?"

"In on the Resurrection. You know, she helped a man say he was Jesus after his death, and he was a look-alike, and they made up this whole story to bring glory to themselves."

"What in the Holy Trinity gave you that idea, my son?"

"My friends, they both agree on this theory, and I don't know what to believe anymore. I've tried to hold on to my faith, Father, but it's just so hard."

"It seems that your friends need a true teaching from God's word."

"I told them what I believe, and they still don't understand."

"People believe what they want to believe. In these times people have blocked out true discernment and say things like 'Everything you do is acceptable,' which is not true discernment."

"If that's not true discernment, then what is?"

"True discernment comes from God and what the Holy Book says and from nothing else. That is why people are changing their sexuality so much these days. It's not because they can't discern between what is biblically right or wrong or humanly moral or immoral. It's because they do not want to discern; they just want to live the way they want to."

"What do we do, then?"

"We love them and try to understand where they are coming from. Many churches block them out, but as Christians we need to love them and invite them into our churches and help them see that homosexuality is a sin. Some churches and congregations think that homosexuality is worse than murder or adultery and cast out those people. But in reality, it's not. I am not saying that all sin carries the same weight; all I am saying is that we as the church need to step up in that way and accept everybody no matter what background."

"Is that why my friends are confused?"

"Your friends aren't confused, Bryan. They just lack the understanding to make a discerned decision; people can't discern if they do not first understand."

"So what you are saying is that I need to give them the knowledge to understand where I am coming from and then allow them to make up their own minds?"

"It is like this we plant the seed of the gospel, and then if your friends accept it, then you can watch it grow in their life, but they can also reject it. It is their choice, much like it was your own once."

"Father?"

"Yes, Bryan."

"How do I know the gospel is true?"

"I think it's best to answer that question with a question: Why do you not believe it is?"

"I guess because recently it has become more and more apparent that it was made up."

"Let me ask you this, then: Do you think that the disciples would die for something that wasn't true?"

"What? No, that would be stupid."

"Do you think apostle Paul went to prison, then was stoned, then was beheaded for a lie?"

"No, that would be horrible; you would have said it was a lie to save your own skin."

"That's how we know Jesus really died and rose and was who he said he was—his followers didn't slip up and say it wasn't true when all those bad things started happening to them; they stood their ground and believed until their very last breath. Why, it's simple actually, because it just is simply true."

"What about science and religion—which one is true?"

"My personal belief is that they intersect because science and its research can help prove Christianity is true."

"I think that's right."

"I don't think that science is wrong; I think it is an interpretation of the way God designed the universe."

"I think it is hard to think of God in the ways of science because God is so vast, and I think we can't really comprehend it."

"You're right; you can't really put God under a microscope. We need to stop trying to maximize our lens to see a small picture of him; we need to widen our field of view."

"Father?"

"Yes?"

"What if the end is coming?"

"The end will come, but only when God the Father allows it. Why are you afraid of the end-times?"

"I am kind of afraid because I don't have a family of my own yet, and I would really like one before the end. You know, meet a nice godly woman and get married and watch my kids grow up."

"Bryan, don't worry, because God is with you until the end of the age, and God knows what time is right."

"Father?"

"Yes?"

"Do you believe in conspiracy theories?"

"Not necessarily. Why do you ask, Bryan?"

"Well, Father, there is this code my friends and I have been trying to figure out, and it's driving me insane."

"What is this code for?"

"Well, Father, it's kind of complicated."

"Try to explain it to me then."

"The code we believe is leading to the end."

Bryan sighed and then continued. "We believe the code is from the Freemasons."

Father Charles stood up and walked silently to the stained glass window where he had previously stood just moments before Bryan had entered.

Bryan looked up and then toward Father Charles, whose back was facing him as he peered out through the colorful stained glass.

Bryan could see the light reflection of Father Charles's face in the window. His face, however, was not holding up a smile as a small light grin emerged from his face.

"The Freemasons are not welcome here; they are a disgrace to the Catholic Church and the world!"

"Is that because they left and made up their own religious protestant groups?"

Father Charles turned around, sighed and then began to speak again. "The Freemasons never liked our doctrine, so they made up their own, not by creating other Protestant groups but by creating degrees and levels and disgracing the Bible by using it in their confounded rituals."

"Is that why you hate them?"

"I don't hate anyone, and we should be excepting, I know, but that is why a pope declared long ago that we were not to engage in such meaningless endeavors."

"Is that why the Catholic Church cast them out?"

"Yes, conspiracy theories, Freemasons, Illuminati— they are all the same meaningless organizations and ideas with no true purpose and are never allowed in the church. They will lead people astray, and that is not what we need!"

"What is it that we need, then, Father?"

"We need people to stop joining these groups, and as for your code that you and your friends are trying to break, don't break it—just leave it alone. It will only cause you harm."

Bryan got up from the pew and thanked Father Charles. "Thank you, Father, for your input and your position, but I am going to have to leave now."

"Very well. You don't have to agree with me, you know, but God has put you on a separate journey, and I am doing my best on my own journey, so please don't hold what I have said against you.

"I won't, Father. I will cherish you and your teachings always."

"I hope you find whatever it is you're looking for, Bryan, and peace be with you always," said Father Charles.

Bryan turned and walked out the door of the chapel and down the steps to meet the black sedan that had pulled back around.

Bryan got in, and the group began the trek back to CIA headquarters to coordinate and connect all the dots to the complex puzzle that had been coming together in Bryan's head ever since he had been held at gunpoint three weeks earlier.

CHAPTER 10

MAGNIFICENT MONUMENT

B ryan, Julie, Tyler, and the director got out of the car at the front of CIA headquarters and entered in the building again. The group sat at a circular glass table in a small room. This room, too, was surrounded by glass walls. The director glared around the table, looking at the three young adults and then carefully at Bryan.

"Mr. Stringer, you haven't been wrong so far; what is our next move?" asked the director. Bryan sat up in his chair at the table. "I have been thinking about this puzzle in my head for a while now, and I think I have it mostly solved," replied Bryan.

"OK, let's hear it, then," said the director.

"Well, our last clue was the US bills. On them was 'In God We Trust,' and that connects to the tapestry because of the clue we found in the Masonic temple in DC: 'Trust the tapestry; the resurrection is near.' And that clue led us to the tapestry of Jesus's resurrection in the Vatican Museum," said Bryan.

"We talked to that tour guide, too, remember?" said Julie.

"What tour guide?" asked the director.

"We asked a tour guide what the connection was between the tapestry and a religious or historical artifact," replied Bryan.

"And what did he or she say?" asked the director.

"She just said it was connected to the ark of the covenant," replied Bryan.

"Oh, really," said the director. She laughed and then continued. "So, like Indiana Jones?"

"Well, once the tour guide explained it to me, it all made sense," said Bryan.

"Oh, OK, what did she say?" asked the director.

"She said that the ark was supposedly connected to the tomb by the way of the town of Emmaus, where the ark of the covenant was supposedly placed and also where Jesus walked after the Resurrection," said Bryan.

"OK, continue," said the director.

"The ark of the covenant was supposedly still held at Aksum in the Saint Mary of Zion cathedral, but I did a quick Google search and read an article that said the ark had been moved from that location in the 1970s due to riots and death threats from many people and groups," said Bryan.

"OK, so where does that leave us?" asked the director.

"Well, my overall theory is that the Freemasons are going to control the US government by using the ark of the covenant's holy power," said Bryan.

"OK, that doesn't sound plausible at all," responded Tyler.

"Why is that?" asked Bryan. Bryan got cut off by Julie insisting that they not get into another fight, so they decided to just skip that discussion altogether. The group heard a knock at the glass door; it was an agent. The director waved the agent in, and the agent placed a file on the table. It was the one from Bryan's house, full of Freemason history.

"Thank you, Greg," said the director.

The agent left the room, and the group opened up the file. Bryan began to explain how the Freemasons have been building the country for their true purpose. "The Freemasons, as you know, are a secret society," said Bryan.

"But we already know that; tell us something that we don't know!" replied Tyler.

"OK, well, I'll tell you something—the Freemasons brought the first African American people over to the United States and turned them into slaves; did you know that? Or did you know that those slaves were whipped and beaten by their white slave owners for no reason or that the slaves built the Washington Monument? Huh, did you know that?"

"OK, OK, sorry," replied Tyler, shrinking down in his chair, somewhat ashamed.

"Let's all take a deep breath and try to understand each other and the different views at the table," said the director.

"What are you, my therapist? asked Tyler in a strong tone.

"She's just trying to help," replied Bryan softly.

"Shut it!" replied Tyler in a loud, trembling voice. He stood up and was about to speak.

"Sit down, or I'll have you arrested!" demanded the director. The director continued as Tyler sat down. "Now what were you going to say, Bryan?"

"I just think we need to face up to our history because with the death of George Floyd and other African Americans, we're all just fighting, not necessarily for the rights of America but for basic human rights that we all deserve. I was watching on the news that an African American man made a white woman drop down on her knees and make her proclaim that she was a murderer because of her so-called white privilege," said Bryan. "But the crazy part was that that lady was carrying home groceries and just living her life, and that African American man who made her do that was doing the exact same thing that the whites did in the South when they brought slaves over. The man was torturing her because of her skin color, and that's dead wrong no matter what color you are."

"That's insane," said Julie. Tyler sat there with tears in his eyes but tried not to let it show as Bryan went on.

"People think that we have to continue this color war, but the only color we're spewing is red—red blood shed by people of all races, colors, religions, and creeds. But at the end of the day, we're just people, humans just fighting for a way to be heard.

"My point is that we're all humans and we shouldn't be divided; we should come together because at the end of the day, we're one race—the human race—and to be honest, that's the only race that truly matters."

"So are you saying we can't live out our heritage or cultural roots?" asked the director.

"No, I'm not saying we shouldn't be proud of where we came from; I am just saying we should just all accept that those bad things happened and try our best as a nation to not make those mistakes again," said Bryan.

"You know, it's ironic that we are called the United States of America yet we're the most divided nation in the world," said Julie.

"Yeah, but I believe it just starts with one person helping people though love and respect and asking people, 'How can I pray for you?' Bringing people together not to fight but to say, 'I accept our history, our true history, with all our faults and mistakes' and say, 'That's not where I want to be; I want to make a change,'" replied Bryan. "I'm so sorry, man." Tears flowed down Bryan's face. He walked around the table and hugged Tyler.

"It's all right, man," replied Tyler.

"I feel so ashamed," said Bryan.

"It's OK, buddy; that wasn't your fault," replied Tyler.

"Yes, it was—it was all my fault. I'm so sorry," said Bryan.

"Bryan, hey, that was your ancestors, not you. You need to stop carrying the weight of the world on your shoulders," said Tyler.

Bryan stopped crying and looked up at Tyler.

"You are forgiven," said Tyler.

Bryan walked back to his seat and began to continue with the Freemason history in his file. He sniffled and continued. "Now it was rumored that the Freemasons were also responsible for the nine-eleven attack along with Saudi Arabian influence."

"Why would they attack their own nation?" asked Julie.

"Well, I believe that they did it to cause confusion, and they wanted Osama bin Laden to take the blame; they wanted the US government to kill him off because he was supposedly a threat to their global expansion plan. Everything the government does affects the Freemasons and the global economy. The Freemasons affect the government and the economy; it is just a cause-and-effect scenario," replied Bryan.

"What do you mean by 'the economy'?" asked the director.

"Well, it's actually in Revelations 13:16 through 13:17: 'Also it causes all both small and great, rich and poor, both slave and free to be marked on the right hand or forehead, so that no one can buy or sell unless he has the mark, that is, name of the beast or the number of its name.' So, I think that once the Freemasons establish this one-world global nation, they will set up a new nation with a new global trading policy," said Bryan confidently.

"What do you mean?" asked Tyler.

"Well, I believe that it will be digital because in the Bible it talks about a cashless society, and we are basically there; and plus, with the creation of Bitcoin and Ethereum and apps like Coinbase and crypto websites, we would only be able to buy and sell digitally. The only thing that we are missing is the removal of cash altogether, and then we will be fulfilling a biblical prophecy," said Bryan.

"So what you are saying is that the United States is being controlled by a secret society behind the scenes," said the director.

"Yes, exactly, and they are probably bringing forth the Antichrist," replied Bryan.

"How do we stop them?" asked the director.

"I don't know yet," said Bryan. "The Antichrist will use technology to disrupt humanity; it might be like a futuristic type of social media or other types of things like websites that spread false news, or it could be some tool that we don't even have yet."

"So are you saying that social media is bad?" asked Tyler.

"No, not at all. I am just saying that social media in the past has disrupted governments and could slowly be destroying democracy itself because it doesn't have parameters," said Bryan.

"How do you know so much about this?" asked the director.

"I watched this documentary a while back called *The Social Dilemma*; it's really good," replied Bryan.

"Oh yeah, I saw that documentary too; it talked all about how the people who work on social media sites don't let their kids use them because of the techniques they use to try to keep you hooked on," replied Tyler.

"OK, ladies and gentlemen, can we please get back to the problem at hand? Thank you," said the director.

"All right, sorry," replied Bryan. "There is one clue we haven't even touched yet."

"You mean the objects in the cornerstone?" asked Julie.

"Yeah," replied Bryan.

Bryan asked the director if he could see the objects, and the director complied. The objects were all laid out on a small metal rectangular serving tray, and Bryan began to examine the clues.

He first looked at the green marble all-seeing eye and examined the semitranslucent triangle. Bryan lifted it up, looking at the back of the triangle, and held it up to the sunlight blazing into the room. He saw coordinates lightly engraved on it. "It reads 38.8895 north and 77.0353 west."

The director wrote the numbers on a small notepad.

"Tyler, will you look up the coordinates on Google Earth on your phone?" asked Bryan.

"Yeah," said Tyler. Tyler googled the coordinates and discovered they corresponded to the Washington Monument. "No way," he said.

"What?" asked Bryan.

"It pulled up the Washington Monument," replied Tyler.

Bryan set the green marble triangle down and picked up the second object, the brown leather book, which had the words "In God We Trust" on it. He put the book on the glass table and then opened it to display five names: George Washington, Benjamin Franklin, John Adams, John Handcock, and Thomas Jefferson.

"OK, we have five names; what do they mean?" asked Bryan.

"It could mean five, as in the number," said Julie.

"Or it could mean the fifth page; check the fifth page," said the director.

Tyler cut the director off. "It's a letter-to-number cipher."

"That's where you change the letter to a number, right?" asked Bryan.

"Yeah, duh, that's why they call it a letter-to-number cipher," replied Tyler.

"Can I borrow your notepad, Director?" asked Bryan. The director slid the notepad and pen over to Bryan's side of the table. Bryan wrote down the five names vertically on the pad and then wrote the corresponding number next to the letter in the alphabet.

"Next we need to do is add up the number in each column," said Tyler. Bryan pulled out his phone and used a calculator to calculate the amount in each column and wrote the sum at the bottom of the pad. "The numbers are 187, 153, 85, 106, and 152," said Tyler.

"The total is 683," said Bryan.

"Great. Now divide 683 by the number of names, which is five," said Tyler.

"OK, then we get 136.6," said Bryan.

"But how does that connect to the Washington Monument?" asked Julie.

"We need a map," said Bryan.

"I will do you one better," said the director. She took a laptop from her bag and pulled up a live satellite image.

"Now if we type 'Washington Monument' into the search bar and we use the ruler tool and measure that distance from the monument out, 136.6 feet, the ark should be right here," said Bryan, pointing.

"Wait, how do you know it's in feet?" asked Tyler.

"Well, when we searched for the cornerstone, it was in feet," said Bryan.

"OK, that works, but what if we're wrong?" asked Tyler.

"Well, let's just hope we're not," said Bryan.

"So what do we do now?" asked Julie.

"Well, since the tapestry is connected to the ark's location, then maybe we bring it and—I don't know—lay it in front of it or something, or maybe some magic can somehow happen. Let's just hope and pray that something happens," replied Bryan.

"I doubt praying will help us, but if you think that's where it is, I will back you up," said Julie.

"All right, but we will have to do it at midnight because there are tourists all day and some in the early evening," replied the director.

"All right, then, let's go find the ark of the covenant," said Bryan with a confident look.

CHAPTER 11

TWISTING TIDES

That night Bryan, Julie, Tyler, and the director drove down to the Washington Monument. Tyler and Julie got out of the van they had driven in and waited for the director and Bryan to get out.

"Director, can I ask you something?" asked Bryan still in the van.

"Yes, Bryan, but quickly because we have to get out of the van and unroll the tapestry because Tyler and Julie are waiting on us."

"All right, um, so I was talking to Julie a while back, and she said it was OK to be different. Is that true? I just want another opinion."

"Being different is good, Bryan. I was an army brat growing up, and that's a little different."

"What if I'm scared to be different? What if I don't want to be myself? What if I just want to be somebody else?"

"Why would you say that?"

"I can never seem to get a girlfriend, and that's always bugged me because Tyler was always the one who got all the girls."

"I know that would be frustrating if I was in your position, but you will find her eventually, and if you don't, then that is God's will for you."

"All right, fine." Bryan sighed and tried to accept and understand what the director was saying to him.

I know you may not be happy about it, but maybe your purpose doesn't allow for a girl in your life right now because they may just distract you from what you were truly meant to do."

"Yeah, I guess you're right."

"Bryan, look around. You may not have a girlfriend like Tyler does, but you may have something better."

"What is that?"

"The open arms of friendship."

"Seriously."

"Come on, Bryan. People need you more than you think. Look at Tyler out there. I mean he probably wouldn't have been able to solve this code without you or at least get this far. Besides, you two are the best of friends. You two may fight sometimes, and there will be disagreements, but inside all that fighting, it just simply means you both care for each other."

"Yeah, you're right. Thanks, Director. That means a lot."

"Anytime. Now let's get out of the van and get back to the others."

Just as the two finished speaking, a second van pulled up behind them.

Four CIA agents got out of the second van, all in black combat uniforms, and started removing the resurrection of Jesus tapestry from it. The group watched as the rolled-up, priceless object was carried all the way from the street to the monument's front entrance. The agents set the tapestry on the ground and waited for orders from the director.

"Move it back until the measuring app says 136.6 feet from the front," yelled the director. Three of the agents lifted the tapestry once again on their shoulders while the other one pulled out his phone and used a measuring app to calculate where the three were supposed to move the tapestry. The group finally set it down in the right spot and then unraveled the large woven work of art fully until it glimmered in the moonlight.

The four agents left soon after being dismissed by the director. Bryan, Julie, Tyler, and the director were circling around the tapestry counterclockwise, looking for the answer that would lead them to the ark. Julie looked back at the monument. "Maybe we need to see it from a different angle," she said.

"I will go up into the monument to get a better look; you three stay here," said the director. She handed Bryan a radio and then went out of sight into the stairwell of the monument.

The director peaked out of a small window at the top of the monument. The director realized that Jesus's eyes in the tapestry were pointing left, toward moonlight and a beam of light. The beam was only visible above because it only seemed like a glare up close. "Bryan, there is a beam of light; I need you to follow it," announced the director.

"Roger that," replied Bryan.

The director made Bryan move diagonally along the beam line until it reached its end. Bryan started to dig.

"I will be down in a moment," said the director though the radio. The group grabbed some small shovels that they had brought with them and began to dig.

Julie pulled a pistol out of the back of her pants and pointed it at Bryan and Tyler.

"Julie, what are you doing!" asked Tyler in extreme shock.

"I am not who you think I am. Why are you not surprised, Bryan? Because Tyler's shocked as hell," said Julie tauntingly.

Bryan stood there with his mouth shut and a small smile on his face. "I'm not surprised because you gave yourself away many times," declared Bryan.

"How?" asked Julie.

"When we were decoding the declaration, you said it was from a Freemason even before we knew that piece of information, and when we were in the library of the Freemason temple, you were stalling on finding the book, so you got suspicious for a moment that I might catch on to your plan; I got mad at Tyler to throw you off, and it worked," said Bryan.

"Well done, Mr. Stringer," replied Julie. Julie clapped her hands slowly and methodically while still holding the gun.

"Now who are you, really?" asked Bryan.

"I am an ancestor of the gnostic people," replied Julie. Tyler just stood there in complete bewilderment at the changes in Julie happening right before his very eyes. He started to cry. A large black limousine drove up, and a tall man got out; it was the president of the United States.

The president walked toward the group; as he got closer, Bryan realized that he was wearing a Masonic necklace around his neck—gold with a triangle-like compass and corner ruler representing the square. Bryan instantly recognized the main Masonic symbol. He also wore an intricately woven apron around his waist full of Masonic symbols and designs. The president stood there, and Julie turned and joined him.

"You're a Freemason?" asked Bryan, somewhat shocked.

"I am, and Mr. Stringer, you have caused quite a stir with your antics. I now must turn up the clock and accelerate my time table; dig it up!" said the president demandingly.

Four Secret Service agents dug into the ground where the students had originally started digging. "Are you the Antichrist?" asked Bryan.

"No, I am a prophet simply doing the devil's handi-work," said the president.

Tyler finally spoke, in a low whimper. "Julie, why are you doing this? Please, please come back to me, please." Through all the stress, noise, and thoughts inside his head, Tyler slowly began to weaken and to bawl.

"I never loved you, your life is a mistake, and don't you realize I used you? You're nothing more than an ant under my foot. Not even God could save you now," said Julie in a roaring tone. Julie laughed hysterically as Tyler began to break down. "You actually cared for me—what a mistake."

Tyler's body trembled in fear, his lips quivered, and endless tears kept falling from his face.

"That's enough!" yelled Bryan.

"Now let's all get down to business while my men are digging. Mr. Stringer, you and I have some things to discuss," said the president.

"Well, the CIA director is in the Washington Monument, and she will shoot you; actually, she should have been down by now," said Bryan.

"Well, Julie took her gun, and she is now locked in the Washington Monument with no way of escape, and my men might throw some tear gas in there, just to make it fun," replied the president tauntingly. Bryan gave him an angry look. "What did you think I was going to do? Smile and give her flowers? Grow up and join the real world," said the president.

"What are you doing?" asked Bryan.

"I am setting up the end," declared the president.

"Julie said she is a gnostic person; are they working with you? You know, the Freemasons?" asked Bryan.

"No, though Julie is," said the president.

"Why?" asked Bryan.

"She believes in the gnostic gospels, and we recruited her mother to uncover the ark at Aksum, which was guarded by one monk; she killed the monk and became its keeper and carried it secretly to this location, at the Washington Monument. Julie, her daughter, now guards it," said the president.

"I don't believe in the gnostic gospels," said Bryan.

"So you believe what? You believe just in what your church tells you?" said the president.

"Well, actually no; there have been many preachers and churches that teach false things, and I choose to believe the Bible as my discernment and my ultimate source of truth," said Bryan.

"What is true truth, then?" asked the president.

"True truth is being able to discern between positions; our own experience and personal outlook on the world make things true to us, but our deepest convictions carry the strongest weight," replied Bryan boldly.

"What does that even mean?" asked the president.

"It means that our own personal experiences make us who we are. For example, when I became a Christian and I stepped out in faith and asked Jesus into my heart, something changed. On the inside I felt different, and I can't quite explain it. Other people have felt it as well. That feeling is the personal relationship with Jesus, and that's nothing I could have ever done on my own; we can't be our own savior," said Bryan.

"You're wrong. I am a servant of the Antichrist. He is my savior, and I am a follower of him. He has dominion over this world, and soon he will rise again. I will make sure of that, and you will bow down and worship him," declared the president.

"What are you going to do to me if I don't?" asked Bryan.

"You will die, but I must first accomplish the task given to me by the dragon himself; then I must pass it on to the beast when the time is right," said the president.

"And by the beast you mean the Antichrist?" asked Bryan.

"Yes, that is precisely what I mean," said the president.

"How are you going to accomplish it?" asked Bryan.

"I am going to use the ark of the covenant to get it under my power and then give it to the beast to honor the serpent by it. Every nation will obey it; he will rebuild the temple as it is written in the scriptures, and it will all be fulfilled," said the president.

"Where are you going use this power?" asked Bryan.

"We have the G7 summit at Camp David where all the other world leaders will come together, and with them under my power and control, the serpent will be glorified. Soon after we will unleash hell on Israel in the final battle, which has already been written," replied the president with his pupils glowing red like flames.

The Secret Service agents finished digging up the ark, and the president looked back at them. "Let's go, gentlemen. Oh, by the way, Mr. Stringer, if you interfere with the serpent's plan, you will die. Let this be a warning!" said the president. He, the Secret Service agents carrying the ark, and—sadly—Julie left in the darkness of night to fulfill what the Freemasons had planned for centuries: the end of all humanity itself.

CHAPTER 12

HUMANITY'S UNDOING

B ryan walked over to Tyler and comforted him with a bro hug. "Thanks, man," said Tyler. "Any time. Now let's go get the director out of the monument," replied Bryan.

The two rushed over to the monument and pulled on the door handle; it wouldn't budge. Bryan banged his fist against the door. "Director, are you OK?" Bryan screamed though the metal door. He heard no answer.

"Shhh! Listen, Bryan," said Tyler, pulling his fist away from the door. The two listened and heard a small clinking sound coming from the inside of the security door. Bryan once again banged on the door three times and waited in silence. The two suddenly heard three bangs from the other side.

"Yes, she's alive!" said Bryan in great relief. "Help me bust this door down."

"I will do you one better," replied Tyler.

"How so?"

"The door to the security room is electrically operated and can only be accessed by keycard."

"Can you get into the wiring and disable the lock?"

"I'll try, but it's going to be hard."

"Well, don't you have that pocket knife?"

"No, they took it away from me when we when we were under arrest at the CIA, but I think I can just bust open the sensor panel since it's plastic."

"I thought you said it was going to be hard."

"It will be without any tools, but I got this."

Tyler pulled the black sensor plate from the wall with Bryan's help and dug his hands into the sides of the sensor plate, slowly prying it open. Two minutes of prying went by when a crack of the back plastic was heard. Tyler then began tampering with the wiring inside, and after a couple of tries, the door unlocked. Bryan ran in and pulled the director out; she was coughing. There was a yellow gas field around them—tear gas.

"The damn president, I ought to get him impeached," said the director, still coughing; her eyes were slightly red and her veins bulging due to her encounter with the gas.

"You OK, Director?" asked Tyler.

"Yes, I'm fine—I can handle a little tear gas," replied the director. "What's next?"

"Well, the president is now apparently the false prophet, so we have to stop him from using the ark of the covenant's holy power at the G7 conference and manipulating all of the other global leaders," said Bryan.

"Where is the conference being held?" asked Tyler.

"Camp David, in Maryland," replied Bryan.

"You mean the presidential retreat?" asked Tyler.

"Yeah, but for us to stop him, we're going to have to break in," replied Bryan.

"Come on, we already broke into the Vatican Museum; I think that's enough breaking and entering for me, thank you," responded Tyler.

"Oh, that reminds me—I have to call some of the agents at the office to pick up the tapestry that's on the ground over there so it doesn't get damaged. Excuse me," said the director. The CIA director walked away from Bryan and Tyler. Then the two came up with a plan for entering the president's retreat.

"Bryan, I really think this is a bad idea," said Tyler.

"Relax, it's probably less penetrable than Fort Knox," replied Bryan.

"Oh, great. Thanks," replied Tyler sarcastically.

"Come on, we have to do this. It's for everybody who isn't doing this. If you go, you could possibly persuade Julie to get back together with you," said Bryan, using his persuasion skills.

"No. Julie and I are done; the truth is too hard to bear. She...she never cared about me in the first place; she was just using me to block us from discovering the ark; that's why she was a tour driver around the monument. She never truly loved me," replied Tyler with tears rolling down his face.

"It's OK, buddy," said Bryan, hugging Tyler for a moment of comfort and then letting go. Tyler wiped his tears away.

"Relationships are hard, but you just have to let her go because if she truly appreciated you, she would not have stabbed you in the back and lied to your face about her true motivations."

"Yeah, I guess you're right."

"So you up for the plan?"

"Yeah, let's do it."

The director got off the phone. "OK, they are coming to pick up the tapestry; what's the plan?" she asked.

"We need a map of Camp David," said Bryan.

"I have one in my car," replied the director.

"Why do you have one in your car?" asked Bryan.

"It's more of a pamphlet, really; the president's staff gave it to me because all of them went on a retreat there; it was supposed to be some type of decompression from work slash group-building training course," said the director.

Bryan, Tyler, and the director walked to her car, and she dug though her glove box and found a yellow pamphlet. The director opened it, and a map of the camp glistened as the sun rose over the sky and night slowly became day.

The director placed the pamphlet outside the window of her car. She then grabbed a pen from her white pantsuit and began to circle things and draw paths on the pamphlet map.

"OK, so the easiest way to sneak into Camp David is to go over the fenced area here, left of the entrance road, and get on the nature trail. Once there, you'll go past the putting green and then to the Aspen Lodge—that is where the president is most likely holding the conference. Then I will enter through the main gate, because I have the security clearance, and drive up from the gate house to the Aspen Lodge; you'll put the ark in the back of the truck, cover it with a tarp, and then we're home free," said the director.

"All right, let's do it," replied Bryan with excitement.

* * *

The group drove an hour and thirty minutes, and the director parked about a mile away from Camp David. "OK, there is a dealership about thirty minutes from here. I am going to get a truck and ditch this car. When you're ready to bring the ark out, signal me with this beeper," said the director. She gave Bryan the small circular disk with a button in the center and a string attached to it. Bryan put it around his neck.

"What happens if we get caught?" asked Tyler.

"Don't. Now go," replied the director.

Bryan and Tyler got out of the director's car and ran onto a nearby trail covered by trees and shrubbery while the director drove off into the distance. Bryan and Tyler were on edge like never before heading up the trail, and the two got to a crossroads with a sign that read To Putting Green. Bryan pointed to the sign. Tyler nodded, and the two went up the trail.

"So what happens when we get to the lodge?" asked Tyler.

"We stop the president's conference," replied Bryan.

Suddenly two men in a dark suits jumped at them from behind. Bryan and Tyler were both knocked out and then carried to a small cabin. Tyler's vision and hearing came back for just a moment, and he caught the word "elm" coming from one of the men in the suits and realized that they were Secret Service agents. Then Tyler's eyes were filled with utter darkness. When the two college students awoke, they were being kept in some type of small storage cabin.

"What happened?" asked Bryan, rubbing his head.

"I think it was those Secret Service agents," replied Tyler.

"You *think*?" asked Bryan.

"Well, things got kinda blurry, OK!" declared Tyler.

"All right, all right, there's no point in arguing now; we just have to figure out how to get out of here," said Bryan.

The cabin had shovels and a shelf with an old car battery and jumper cables, cans of spray paint, and a big metal barrel. There were two doors, one in the front fully covered in wood, and a Dutch-style door in the back; both were locked from the outside. Tyler opened the top of the Dutch door, but sadly it was barred.

"At least we get some fresh air," said Bryan.

"We're never getting out of here!" replied Tyler.

"Yes, we are; we just gotta think," said Bryan.

Tyler paced back and forth across the wood-beamed floor.

"Do you have any quarters?" asked Bryan.

"Yeah. Why? What would you need quarters for?" asked Tyler.

"I have an idea," replied Bryan. Tyler pulled out a number of quarters from his pocket and handed them to Bryan. Bryan got the car battery and placed it by the back door and opened the top of the door, revealing the bars.

Bryan then stacked two quarters together and connected them to one end of the jumper cable and connected the other end to the car battery.

"What are you doing?" asked Tyler.

"I'm getting us out of here," replied Bryan. He touched the coin contraption to the cool metal bars, and sparks flew.

"Oh, I get it—you made a homemade electrical saw," said Tyler.

"Yeah, I'm cutting though the metal bars with the quarters." Bryan cut the top of the bars and then the bottom. He then began kicking the loose bars with his feet until the cylinder shards fell out the open window. Tyler and Bryan squeezed themselves out of the window and onto the outside grass.

"Where are we exactly?" asked Bryan.

"Well, before I fully blacked out, I heard the Secret Service say something about the word 'elm.'" said Tyler.

"Oh well, that makes sense because the Elm Shed is right next to the Aspen Lodge," said Bryan.

"Well, let's stop the president, then," replied Tyler.

"No, the place is too well guarded," said Bryan.

"When a place is too well guarded, then what better way to get in than to be a guard?" replied Tyler.

Moments later Bryan and Tyler knocked out the two Secret Service agents who were guarding them by hitting them on the back of the head with two shovels they had found in the shed. The two unconscious men were then pulled into the shack, tied up, and undressed; Tyler and Bryan put on their uniforms.

The two college students walked out with earpieces in their ears and nice dressy suits. They traveled the short distance to the president's lodge. They approached the big brown wooden doors of the lodge and entered quietly. The lodge was beautiful; the high-beamed ceilings and wood paneling were glimmering. You could hear the president's voice in the other room, as well as other voices.

Bryan and Tyler walked closer to a flash of bright golden light, and when they turned the corner, they saw a brown circular table; seated there were the seven global leaders. Beside the table was the ark, open, with a bright, glimmering light shining out of it. Papers from the circular desk were flying everywhere in the air, and there stood the president, clothed in an embroidered tunic, with Julie beside him. Loud crashes like thunder emanating from the ark filled the room.

"Stringer, you come any closer, and I will kill her," said the president holding a knife to her neck.

"You don't have to do this, sir—you're the president," said Bryan.

"No, I'm not the president any longer; I'm the false prophet, the one who will start a global war against Israel, the one who possesses God's power," said the president.

The president's capillaries slowly turned black. "The end is near, Bryan Stringer. You can't stop it now for it is written in the book that if you stop me, you still start the beginning of the end."

"No one can contain God's full power, not even you!" declared Bryan. The two men moved toward the false prophet with the air around the room pushing against them like a trillion windstorms.

"Shut it! Shut it!" yelled Bryan.

"No," yelled the false prophet.

Julie bit the false prophet's arm, he screamed and dropped the knife, and she slammed the ark's lid shut; the wind ceased.

CHAPTER 13

POWER AND CONTROL

T wo Secret Service agents ran into the room and tackled the false prophet. "On behalf of the United States of America, you have the right to remain silent," said one of the Secret Service agents.

"What? I didn't do anything wrong!" said the false prophet.

"I'm sorry, Mr. President. I just heard from the CIA director that you have stolen a tapestry from the Vatican Museum. The director believes you were going to use that tapestry to send a coded message to the Arabs, therefore committing treason against the United States government," said the other agent. The two agents placed cuffs on his hands, and his black eyes returned to their normal color.

He gazed up at Bryan and Tyler as he was led away and said, "Mr. Stringer, the beast will get you for this; I promise you that."

Bryan and Tyler then looked at the rest of the world leaders. The prime minister of Canada said, "He asked us to give him the nuclear codes for all of our countries."

"Did you give them to him?" asked Tyler.

"We had no choice; he threatened us with the ark," replied the prime minister of Germany.

"Right before you two came in, he initiated a multi-missile attack," said the prime minister of France.

"On what target?" asked Tyler.

"Israel," replied the prime minister of Italy.

"Well, can we stop it?" asked Bryan.

"I don't know," said the prime minister of Canada.

Bryan and Tyler whispered quietly, away from all of the world leaders.

"Well, that's reassuring," said Tyler.

"Tell me about it," replied Bryan.

The world leaders called their military commanders and told them to shoot heat-seeking flares up in the air to combat the heat-seeking missiles and draw them away from Israel. The vice president walked in. "What's the situation, and why is the ark of the covenant on a table?"

"It's a long story, sir," replied the secretary.

"Sir, the president launched a global nuclear attack against Israel," said the military commander.

"OK, what are our options?" asked the vice president.

"Sir, all six other nations just did a counterstrike trying to stop the missiles from hitting Israel," said the commander. The leaders were all watching the missiles on a small television in the office. The group watched as the missiles were redirected in the air by the counterartillery. "Three, two, one, detonation!" said the commander. The group in the office screamed and cheered like they were watching their favorite sports team, hugging one another and thanking their gods for what they had done to spare the world from this global monstrosity.

The group then turned their attention to the gold-plated ark of the covenant.

"What are we to do with this?" asked the prime minister of Canada.

"I want it," replied the prime minister of Germany.

"I should have it; it is a religious relic and should go in the pope's archive in the Vatican," said the prime minister of Italy.

"You? Why you?" said the prime minister of Canada.

The group of world leaders fought for control. Though all of the chaos, Bryan and Tyler completely forgot about Julie. "Wait, where is Julie?" asked Tyler.

"Aw, man, you're thinking about her again. See, I told you, you still have feelings for her. See, this is perfect," replied Bryan.

"No, Bryan—she is a fugitive now. We have to find her before the government does, or they will put her in jail for life or sentence her to death for treason," said Tyler.

The CIA director walked into the lodge. "Gentlemen, on behalf of the United States government, we will be taking the ark of the covenant off your hands," said the director. Four CIA agents walked in the door and then picked up the ark by the rods and carried it out and placed it on a gray truck before covering it up with a brown tarp. "No one shall discuss this outside this room," demanded the director.

Bryan and Tyler walked out the door toward the truck, and the director followed them. "What was that whole thing about the president stealing the tapestry?" asked Bryan.

"I may have pulled a few strings. We caught Luis Ivanov, and blaming it on the president, who actually ended up being the false prophet, was just a bonus," replied the director.

"Killing two birds with one stone," said Tyler.

"Exactly, and you never pressed your mini receiver necklace, so I figured I had to make up an excuse to come over here," said the director.

The group got into the truck. "What happens now?" asked Bryan.

"We return the tapestry to Italy's government, getting you three off the hook and framing the president slash false prophet. Oh, by the way, where is Julie?" asked the director.

"Julie ran away amid the distraction of the missile attack," replied Tyler.

"Oh, so she's a fugitive, then," said the director.

"I guess so," said Bryan.

"We'll check it out," said the director.

"Oh, by the way, there are two Secret Service agents that we hit on the head with shovels that need to be revived and untied," said Bryan.

"Where are they?" asked the director.

"They are over there, in the wooden shed," replied Bryan, pointing.

The director called an agent on her walkie-talkie to free the two men.

"What will we do with the ark of the covenant?" asked Tyler.

"We will return the ark to the spot near the Washington Monument where it was originally for safekeeping," said the director.

"But it wasn't originally placed there; Julie took it from Ethiopia," said Tyler.

"I know, but I think it is best if we keep it there. And then we won't cause a full-scale war," replied the director.

CHAPTER 14

GLOBAL PEACE

A week later the president was quietly impeached, and the House and the Senate met together in one room to discuss the president's mental state. The president was taken out of office due to the testimonies of Bryan and Tyler, as well as the CIA director, and no press was allowed any coverage. The six other world leaders were sworn to secrecy about the ark. Sitting there in that room watching the proceedings take place, all were nervous. A day later the former president was sent to a mental treatment facility for trying to take down the United States through treason and its allies through a deadly nuclear missile attack. The whole event was classified, and there was no public record, except for a dossier—and Bryan and Tyler's knowledge, of course. As soon as the former president was taken away, the vice president was sworn in right there in that room.

A press conference was held later that day at the White House to explain to the world that the vice president was now the president, but no one went into full detail about why the former president was replaced except for saying it was due to a mental illness and that it was in accordance with the Twenty-Fifth Amendment.

Bryan and Tyler were standing in the back of the room during the press conference. "Shouldn't we tell them what really happened?" asked Tyler quietly.

"I don't think it's our place to explain what happened," replied Bryan.

The president's officials shut down the questioning and said that they were still evaluating the situation. All the journalists and photographers started getting up and leaving the room. Bryan and Tyler walked back with the CIA director to the Oval Office after the reporters had all left.

Bryan and Tyler sat down on the yellowish-white sofas across from each other in the middle of the room. Moments later the new president walked in and sat down at his wooden desk. "Gentlemen, you should be proud of yourselves; you have stopped the biggest threat America has ever known," said the new president.

"Thank you, sir," replied Bryan.

The president continued, and Bryan whispered to Tyler, "I'm talking to the president, and I am a history student; this is totally going to amp up my grade in that class."

"I thought you were studying religion," said Tyler quietly.

"I am majoring in religion but minoring in history," replied Bryan. The two turned their heads to look at the president, who was still speaking.

"And that is why, gentlemen, you two need to accompany me to Italy as your reward, and since Bryan is studying religion, I figured it would do you good. I already had one of my staff clear it with your dean," said the president.

The CIA director walked in and stood beside the president's desk. "You have been to Italy, haven't you?" asked the CIA director, smiling. The two nodded their heads, trying not to think about the fact that they had stolen the tapestry about two weeks before.

That day the two college students and the president boarded Air Force One and jetted off to Italy. Bryan and Tyler sat down on the comfy leather seats on the plane.

Standing across from Bryan and Tyler was one of the Secret Service agents. He looked vagally familiar, and then Bryan remembered he was one of the men who had attacked him at Camp David. "How are you?" asked Bryan.

The agent didn't answer and stood still with his hands in front of his body.

"Um, excuse me, where is the restroom?" asked Tyler.

The Secret Service agent just pointed to the left.

"Thanks," said Tyler, about to pat the agent on the back, but then he realized that that probably wasn't the best move, turned, and went to go find a bathroom.

Bryan pressed a button to close the blinds and leaned back in his chair and began to take a nap. He later awoke to a stewardess in a blue suit telling him they had five minutes until they landed. Bryan looked over at Tyler as he was eating a pasta dish on a foldout table. "What are you doing?" asked Bryan, slowly waking up.

"I'm eating pasta," said Tyler.

"What? Why?" asked Bryan.

"A man's gotta eat," replied Tyler.

"All right, whatever," replied Bryan, regaining his awareness.

The plane's wheels touched the ground with a screeching noise as they grazed the pavement strip and the presidential plane smoothly came to a halt. The president walked by, and Bryan perked up and got out of his chair and walked over to the exit staircase. As Bryan walked down the airplane staircase, following the president, Tyler followed behind Bryan. There were two black limousine-type cars waiting for them, one for Bryan and Tyler and one for the president.

The president went in one limousine while Bryan and Tyler were driven in the other. They were both taken to the Vatican City and were later joined by the Vatican police force for more security. The two limousines pulled up in front of the Apostolic Palace. The president was let out of his car, and moments later so were Tyler and Bryan. The pope, dressed in all white, was awaiting their arrival. The president shook the pope's hand and introduced Tyler and Bryan. Then the Swiss Guard led them down the hallway and up a flight of stairs and turned a few lefts into the pope's grand library.

There were shelves of books on one side with a painting in the center on the wall and a large woven rug on the floor. Bryan and Tyler sat down in two chairs with many other chairs arranged in a circle around them. The president then sat down next to Tyler and waited for the other religious leaders to come in and sit down. The pope was at the door greeting the leaders as they came in the room one by one.

First came the grand imam of the Sunni Muslims, then came the Dalai Lama of the Buddhist faith, and soon after one more leader entered. He was the lead rabbi of the Jewish faith. After the pope had greeted all the guests, he sat down and began the meeting. "One of the issues we need to deal with is the divisiveness caused by the five major belief systems that are represented in the room today. Basically, all these different beliefs are very similar and should unite us and not divide us," said the pope.

"I agree that all the five belief systems encourage man to be and do better, and those who believe in these system should be treated with respect. However, with due respect, there are significant differences that mean they all can't be true at the same time," replied Bryan.

"Shhhh! Bryan, I brought you here to watch, not intervene," said the president.

"That is an interesting concept, Bryan, but the outcomes of these five competing belief systems are causing destruction in our society, and aren't there more similarities than differences?" asked the pope.

"Well, Your Holiness, may I do a brief compare and contrast between the five belief systems?" asked Bryan.

"Yes, Bryan, but please be brief because we have more important things to attend to," said the pope.

"Four of the belief systems, Catholicism, Protestantism, Judaism, and Islam, are monotheistic. Buddhism believes in finding enlightenment or a holy state, and they find it in themselves, and since man is supposedly sinful, how can Buddhism be true, because you can't fix sin by yourself?

"Those first four have some of the same roots and relationship to the patriarch Abraham in their origins, and all of them believe that man is sinful and separated from their God. They all need a savior to get right with their God and get to an eternal heaven," said Bryan.

"Yes, that is true," replied the pope.

"Again, Buddhism is the odd one out because they believe you just keep suffering, and they have no way to remove the eternal suffering; they want to achieve a goal of enlightenment. But if you are sinful, you need a savior. Buddhism doesn't have a savior, so Buddhism is simply inadequate," said Bryan.

"Well, how is your religion different?" demanded the Dalai Lama firmly.

"Well, first of all, Protestant Christians like me don't have a religion; we have a direct relationship with God through the saving grace of Jesus. In Catholicism, on the other hand, you don't have a direct relationship with Jesus; all you have is a sinful man of power who believes if you do enough good works, if you do more good than bad, you might be saved. But how do you know if you do more good than bad?

"There is no scale to measure your good deeds versus your bad deeds; therefore, Catholicism is inadequate. Why would you ever want to risk your eternity on something you can't measure? In Protestant Christianity you can be sure of your salvation in Jesus because a sinful man cannot save you; only Jesus, who was a sinless man, can save you," said Bryan confidently.

"That is absolutely absurd," exclaimed the pope.

"Since Islam believes they should die for their God, and Judaism believes their savior hasn't come yet, then there truly must be one savior, and that's Jesus."

"That's ridiculous and absurd," said the imam and rabbi.

"So you see, Your Holiness, there are many differences in the five belief systems," said Bryan.

"Bryan, these differences seem very academic and not worth splitting hairs over. We just need them all to get over their differences and get along as one mankind," replied the pope.

"Very well," said Bryan.

"Next on the agenda, if Mr. Stringer is done speaking his untrue, ungrateful mind and unwanted opinions, is addressing the president's concern on the previous president's failure as the supposed false prophet," said the pope.

"Wait a second, how did you know about that?" asked Tyler.

"The Father told me," replied the pope.

"Right," said Tyler, nodding his head in compliance yet half believing.

"Well, sir, this has truly been an honor and a privilege, but Tyler and I must go," said Bryan.

"Where to?" asked the president.

"We are going to go back to the villa that my dad uses for business during the summertime," replied Bryan.

"Where is it?" asked the pope.

"Tuscany," said Bryan.

"That's three hours away; I will have one of my drivers take you," said the pope.

"Thank you, sir," replied Bryan.

"By the way, Bryan, Air Force One is leaving after this meeting, so if you want to stay longer, one of my staff will send you and Tyler plane tickets so you can get back when you're ready," replied the president.

"OK, thank you so much, sir; I really appreciate it," said Bryan. Bryan and Tyler walked out of the palace and got into the car with the driver, and off they went to Bryan's family's chateau in Tuscany.

"Why did you pull me away?" asked Tyler.

"The pope addressed the false prophet," replied Bryan.

"And so what?"

"The pope said the 'supposed false prophet.'"

"I am still not following you?"

"Supposed, a.k.a. not the real one."

"OK, wait, hold on a second—you're telling me the false prophet we stopped was an imposter?"

"More like a decoy."

"For what, though?"

"For the real thing."

"Who?"

"The pope."

Bryan and Tyler drove up to the villa, which was an orangish-tan color. On the left was a pool and a guest house; there were also tall, skinny green trees in front of the pool for some privacy, even though there were only vineyards around and no other houses for miles.

The two got out of the car, each with a small duffel bag. They walked up the orange clay steps onto the patio and then gasped as they saw a tall, tanned figure before them.

CHAPTER 15

GOVERNMENTAL ISSUE

"Gwardo!" said Bryan, puzzled.

"This is my winter palace, and sometimes, when your dad isn't here, my summer palace," said Gwardo, who was wearing colorful swimming trunks.

"Why are you here?" asked Bryan.

"I am here do get what is owed to me," replied Gwardo.

"You mean the tapestry?" asked Tyler.

"Exactly. By the way, where is Julie?" asked Gwardo.

"Julie—Julie was a gnostic and turned on us," said Tyler, teary eyed.

"Terrible, that's just terrible," replied Gwardo with worry on his face.

"Yeah, anyway, we have to get to the main problem at hand," said Bryan.

"Which is?" asked Gwardo.

"The pope," declared Bryan.

"What's wrong with the pope?" asked Gwardo.

"Bryan thinks that the pope is the real false prophet," said Tyler.

"What? That's ridiculous; you're just lying flat out," said Gwardo.

"It's not worth fighting over who's right or wrong; it's all about speaking truth," said Bryan.

The three men went inside the main house. The floor of the house was covered in light-red zigzag tile, and there was white furniture throughout. Bryan went into one of the bedrooms with twin beds. "Now, Gwardo, I will allow you to stay as our guest, so you can take the guest house, and Tyler and I will sleep in these two beds," said Bryan.

"But what about the tapestry?" asked Gwardo.

"You will have it soon enough. Now let's all eat and get ready for bed; we will talk about it in the morning," replied Bryan.

Tyler and Bryan lay down on their beds. "Hey, Bryan, what were you saying about the pope and the false prophet?"

"I was saying that the pope could possibly be the real false prophet."

"What makes you say that?"

"Well, in the Bible the false prophet is said to be the religious leader of the Antichrist and come from Rome."

"How do you know the false prophet we caught was a fake?"

"Well, in Matthew 7:15 it says to beware of false prophets that come to you in sheep's clothing but inwardly are ravening wolves."

"So let's just suppose that the false prophet we caught was a decoy, and let's go with your theory of the pope being the false prophet and see where we get?"

"OK, so let's just say that the pope is the true false prophet. Accordingly what we heard from the pope in that meeting today was true, and they are trying to unite all the world's religions."

"Yeah, but how?"

"By bringing about fear."

"OK, and what make you say that?"

"Well, let's just take critical race theory in America, for example. Satan is trying to break America apart by splitting the church, dividing the races, and causing confusion and creating division within the nation."

"So are you saying that you can't believe in critical race theory and still be a Christian?"

"See, Christianity doesn't have a race; we are followers of God, and God sees us all the same. We should still support Black people because I don't see them as Black; I just see them as people.

"Critical race theory, however, says that if you are white, you are a racist, and if you are not for their organization, you are against all Black people. Therefore white people are wrong in every regard, and we should bow down and kneel before people and say we are sorry because we are white and because of the color of our skin.

"In reality, though, that is the exact same thing that whites did to the Blacks earlier in history. Instead of coming together and stopping racial discrimination altogether, all we are doing is feeding the beast. The color of our skin doesn't make us who we are; it is our moral principles and our character that allow us to be who were supposed to be.

"People are so divided and more worried about political parties and who is going to run the country for the next four years than God himself. You know, whoever the president is it doesn't matter because at the end of the day. Jesus is still king over all of them."

"So are you saying we shouldn't vote?" asked Tyler.

"No, we should vote because it matters. All I am saying is that whoever is in authority over us is by the will of God," said Bryan.

"I still don't believe in God, but what you are saying about critical race theory makes sense because it's logical because we should all love those who look different than us but in reality are the same as us."

"You're right. Critical race theory doesn't even make sense because they are talking about unity but cutting out all the white population. Unity requires everyone, and we should all love each other; that's the truth."

"But there is no peace in critical race theory; all I saw on television was people throwing things and stealing. It wasn't peaceful at all."

"I think we should all take a breath and look at what Martin Luther King Jr. said: 'Peace if possible; truth at all costs.' Is peace possible through the BLM movement? Potentially yes, but we have to search the truth in such a way that is respectful and not violent."

"How are we supposed to bring unity and peace if our government is so messed up?"

"Yeah, there are so many problems. We're moving away from the morals and values that America stood for, but we must remember: 'Peace if possible; truth at all costs.'"

"Exactly, the only reason the federal government was set up was to establish laws and protect us by a creation of an army and military that brought peace."

"How do you know that?" asked Bryan.

"I'm a big military history buff; that's what got me interested in decryption—I have always wanted to work for the CIA, FBI, or military and decode things and make a difference."

"You never told me that when we were in high school."

"Do I have to tell you everything?" asked Tyler. Bryan looked at Tyler and understood that he didn't have to tell him everything and tried to avoid the awkwardness by steering the conversation in another direction.

"We still really don't know who the Antichrist is," said Bryan.

"You're right; it could be anybody," replied Tyler.

"Well, it would have to be someone with endless power."

"Too bad it can't be a government; the government has endless power."

"Tyler, you're a genius." Bryan sat up on his bed, and Tyler followed suit.

"What are you thinking?" asked Tyler.

"What if it's the president?"

"The president—are you crazy? That's ridiculous."

"Well, did you notice that that meeting was only for religious leaders but the president was there?"

"And he's not a religious leader."

"It's plausible that he's the Antichrist."

"Oh my gosh, this feels too real to be true."

"But what if it is?" asked Bryan.

"Do you think that the Freemasons caused the president's rise to power?" asked Tyler.

"It certainly seems plausible, and all the facts add up. I can't even believe this; there is no denying it now."

"So what do we do now?"

"We get some rest and discuss it in the morning," replied Bryan as he turned off the lamp on the bedside table in between the two beds. And as night fell, so did the thoughts in their mind, and the two were out like a light. When they awoke Gwardo was in the kitchen drinking wine and reading a newspaper.

"What are you reading?" asked Tyler.

"I'm reading about the rising tensions in Israel. I hear they are going to have another war," said Gwardo.

"Oh man, who's involved?" asked Tyler.

"Russia is involved, and some Middle Eastern countries. It's not a big deal; they have wars all the time," replied Gwardo.

Bryan went over to the silver fridge in the corner of the room and grabbed the milk, then poured himself a glass. "I made you cornetti; they are on the counter," said Gwardo.

Bryan grabbed one and ate it. "These are really good; how did you make these?"

"From an old recipe book. By the way, I want the tapestry you promised," said Gwardo demandingly.

"I know I promised, and I will ship it back to you," replied Bryan.

"You better!" said Gwardo in a slightly angered tone.

"I will, I will—I promise. Let's all just relax and calm down and take a deep breath," said Bryan.

"Which one are you—my yoga instructor or my therapist?" replied Tyler, laughing. "I'm kidding. By the way, is one of the president's staff sending you the tickets?"

"Yes, I have them in my phone, and we both have our passports, right?" asked Bryan.

Tyler brought out his duffel bag and pulled out a blue passport. "Yep, got it," said Tyler.

"All righty, let's go, then," said Bryan. Tyler and Bryan said goodbye to Gwardo, got into Bryan's dad's small Fiat Panda, and off they went to the airport.

"What airport are we flying out of?" asked Tyler.

"Galilei International, and get ready because it's a connecting flight," said Bryan.

"Oh my gosh, are you stinking serious? I hate those."

"I know you do, but it's either that or stay in Italy."

"Fine," replied Tyler, frustrated. The two got to the airport and took two connecting flights en route to Washington, DC, home.

CHAPTER 16

THE AFTERMATH

After the plane landed, Bryan and Tyler headed to customs. "The first flight was one thing, but the second was just so brutal," said Tyler, exhausted.

"OK, stop complaining; we're here now," said Bryan, annoyed.

"What, are you afraid that my complaining will lead to something dreadful?"

"It already has—you're giving me a headache."

"Sorry."

Bryan and Tyler finished clearing customs and walked out to the parking lot. "What are we going to do about Gwardo and the tapestry?" asked Tyler.

"I don't know; we have to get it from the CIA director first."

Bryan and Tyler walked to a green car. "How are we going to get home? My car is at my house," said Bryan.

"I called an Uber."

"Well, that was a great idea; I'm proud of you."

The driver of the green car rolled down his window. "Where to?" he asked.

"Sorry, sir, we're waiting for an Uber; we don't need your services, so if you could just scoot out of the way, that would be greatly appreciated," said Bryan.

"Um, Bryan, that is our Uber driver," said Tyler.

"Oh."

Bryan and Tyler got in the back of the green car and put there duffel bags on their laps. "Thirty-five fifteen Woodly Road, Cleveland Park, right?" asked the driver. Bryan and Tyler nodded.

"I don't trust this guy," whispered Bryan.

"Why?" asked Tyler.

"Because he drives a light-green car—I mean, who does that?" said Bryan.

"Who finds clues and solves a cipher left by a big, bald Russian guy and brings his friends on an adventure they didn't ask to be on?" exclaimed Tyler.

"Who gets betrayed by his own girlfriend and ends up being an accomplice to the president, who ends up being the decoy false prophet?" said Bryan, holding his position.

"OK, that's not funny; you went too far on that one."

"What do you mean?"

"I'm pretty sure you crossed a line there, bud," said Tyler defensively.

"Hmm, I don't know. I'm pretty sure I hit it right on the nose."

"OK, all right, let's just drop it," said Tyler, frustrated.

Tyler and Bryan were silent the whole car ride after that. They arrived at Bryan's house and got out, paid the driver, and went inside; they fell asleep within minutes due to exhaustion and jet lag. Tyler and Bryan both awoke when they heard loud screaming and a knock at the door. Bryan got up off the couch and opened the door. "Julie?" he said, astonished and bewildered.

Tyler perked up from his awkward sleeping position on the floor and ran to the door. "Julie, what...what are you doing here?"

"I'm here to say goodbye; I'm going underground," replied Julie.

"Why?" asked Tyler.

"Well, the Feds know I'm connected to the crime, and if they find me, I will be convicted," said Julie.

"What are you going to do?" asked Bryan.

"I'm going to hide out. The ark was in my possession, and now I'm the only true gnostic monk that can guard it," said Julie.

"So what now? The US government has the ark; how are you going to get it back?" asked Tyler.

"I found a small group of Freemasons to help me steal it, and now we are on our way to the caves of Israel to place it and guard it in its homeland," said Julie.

"What happens when the director finds out it was you?" asked Bryan.

"She will suspect it's me, and she will come looking, but she won't find me," said Julie. "I can't believe you ran out on us like that!" said Tyler, angered.

"I'm sorry about turning on you; I wish I could have told you who I really was, but it would have gone against the gnostic code," replied Julie.

"Looks like that's the one code I can't break," said Tyler, mumbling under his breath.

"Yeah, well, I better be off. See you around some-time," said Julie.

Bryan and Tyler both nodded as Julie walked out and shut the door. "I don't think I can go back to normal life now," said Tyler.

"What do you mean?"

"She was everything I had."

"Mhmm," said Bryan, coughing.

"What, I meant that in a loving way, and besides, you know I will always be your friend."

"Yep, still not going away. The emotional pain is still there from that comment; it's still floating in the air."

"What do you want me to say?"

"Nothing, nothing."

"What?"

"I have got to get me a girlfriend," replied Bryan.

"Bro, girls are dangerous—hence what you've seen," said Tyler.

"That was just one bad experience."

"OK. That was not a bad experience; it was the worst breakup in the history of breakups. I mean, who in her right mind would betray her country and, more impor-tantly, her boyfriend?"

"Julie would."

"I know. It's ridiculous, it's outrageous, and it's unbe-lievably complicated."

"No, it's not."

"What do you mean?"

"I think you are exaggerating it a little bit."

"I highly doubt that. Oh, and by the way, what if you dated Lilly Grasmere?" said Tyler.

"No, no she would never go for me," replied Bryan.
"Why not?"

"Because she's too attractive."

"And what are you?"

"A man."

"Exactly, you are a man; so be one and go ask her out."

"I don't know, man, after seeing you and Julie's relationship—it would never work."

"Dude, Julie was a traitor to the United States. It doesn't get much worse than that."

Bryan shrugged his shoulders. "Yeah, you're right." Bryan decided to call up Lilly Grasmere and ask her out. He tried to forget all the clues and conspiracies and all that had happened in the past and adjust to normal life again.

* * *

Lilly said yes to Bryan's offer, and he met her the next day at a local coffee shop. And as the next day came, so did his expectations and worries. "Lilly," said Bryan.

"Oh, hi, Bryan. How are you? I haven't seen you since freshman year," said Lilly with a smile.

"Yeah, well, time does fly," replied Bryan with his palms sweating.

"So how have things been? What have you been up to?" asked Lilly.

"Well, I haven't really ever done anything interesting since freshman year—just been going around," said Bryan nervously.

"Come on, that isn't true. You went to Italy with the president because you are studying religion, and you just happened to be picked from your religious class by your dean, right?" asked Lilly.

"Something like that," replied Bryan. As Bryan listened to Lilly talk, he became more entranced with her and more interested in her endeavors. "So you're studying biology now, right?" he asked.

"Yeah, over at the university medicine building."

"Oh, OK. Cool."

"You know what? I don't think this is going to work out," said Lilly in a soft voice.

"Why?" asked Bryan.

"I'm just too busy, and besides, I like you as a friend, and you clearly have a lot going on."

"Uh, OK, I get it."

"OK, bye, Bryan," Lilly said. She got up out of her chair and left the coffee shop. Bryan sat there alone feeling discarded and didn't understand why he could never get a girlfriend. After around five minutes, he got up and decided to walk home. Bryan walked up to his house and through the front door.

"Hey. How was your date?" asked Tyler, intrigued.

"I don't want to talk about it."

"What happened?"

"She wasn't interested; she said she was too busy."

"Well, what I have found out about relationships is that you don't need one to be happy."

"Yeah, I guess," responded Bryan in an unhappy tone.

"Sometimes you just have to accept your fate," said Tyler. Just then an orange envelope slid through the mail slot in the front door.

Bryan turned around, grabbed the envelope, and opened it. "Tyler, come here quick!" said Bryan urgently.

"What is it?"

"It's the dossier of the top secret documents from our discovery of the ark."

"Who sent it?"

Bryan flipped through the pages and then looked at the back of the envelope for the return address. "It's from the central detention facility," he said.

"Oh my God—it's Ivanov," said Tyler, shocked.

"What does he want?"

"Oh, here we go—there is a slip of paper in between the pages."

Bryan flipped through to that page. "It says, 'I will make this public knowledge if you don't get me a trial sooner,'" said Bryan, reading the slip of paper out loud.

"What do we do?"

"We need help." Bryan picked up his phone and dialed a number.

"Who are you calling?" asked Tyler.

"The director."

The phone buzzed for a few moments, and no one answered. Then suddenly they heard three evenly spaced knocks at the door. Bryan hung up the phone, moved closer to the door, and slowly turned the knob. He cracked the door open in hesitation and peered out. It was the director.

"You called," said the director. Bryan opened the door wide for her to walk in and then shut it after her.

"How did you get here so fast?" he asked.

"I was on my way over to congratulate you and see how the religious meeting went," said the director.

"Well, the meeting went great, and Tyler and I stayed in my dad's villa in Tuscany for a night and then left, and here we are," said Bryan.

"How was your date?" asked the director.

"How do you know about that?" asked Bryan.

"We do surveillance for a living; a quaint little coffee shop isn't really a private place, you know. Oh, and by the way, do you know where the ark went? We had it in analysis, and now it's gone," said the director.

"No, no, we do not," said Tyler, holding in his fear.

"Well, if anything comes your way, just let me know," said the director.

"Um, Director, it's Ivanov," replied Bryan. He handed the director the piece of paper and the dossier.

"I guess we will have to move up the trial," said the director.

"What do we do then?" asked Bryan.

"We wait it out. I will call his lawyer and be done with this," said the director.

"Oh, and one more thing. I need a huge favor—I need to borrow the tapestry," said Bryan.

"No. First the ark is stolen, and now you want the tapestry?" said the director.

Bryan and Tyler gave the director a cold, hard stare. "OK, fine, but what are you doing with it?" said the director.

"We're going to ship it back to Italy to the museum. There is a man who works there and who helped us steal it, and he wants it back. We promised him," said Bryan.

"No!" said the director.

"Listen, do you really want the man to call it in and say that the tapestry in Italy right now is a fake? If so, then the authorities will take a closer look at it, and then there will be an international incident. Do you really want that?" asked Bryan tauntingly.

"OK, we will roll it up and ship it; what's the man's name?" asked the director.

"Gwardo Angelo," Bryan replied.

"Right. Again, if you see the ark, please let me know. Oh, and, Tyler, I have a cryptanalyst's internship at the agency, if you want it," said the director.

"OK, when do I start?" asked Tyler.

"Next Tuesday," said the director.

"All right, I'll be there," replied Tyler semiexcitedly.

Bryan opened the door and then closed it once the director left; he leaned against the closed door. "You think she knows?" he asked.

"What, about the ark?" asked Tyler.

"Yeah."

"Well, probably."

"We're so screwed, then," said Bryan, slamming his fist into the door.

The next day Bryan stared at the newspaper in extreme frustration. Tyler came running through the front door. "Bryan, Bryan, did you see it!" he asked.

"Yeah, I did."

Bryan and Tyler read about the secret dossier that had just leaked in the newspaper that morning. "He said if we moved up the trial, he wouldn't leak it, but he did it anyway," said Tyler.

"The worst part is that now we can't go anywhere or do anything. Ugh, this is just like the Pentagon Papers!" said Bryan in frustration.

Just then there was a loud racket outside of Bryan's house. Bryan went to the window and peered out; he saw his neighbors as well as photographers and journalists. They were taking pictures and requesting that Bryan come out. He hesitated and then opened the front door; he stood on his front porch. "Everybody, calm down, please. Nothing has happened; that document is completely false, so please go back inside your homes!" yelled Bryan.

"Mr. Stringer, how do you feel about exposing one of America's greatest mysteries?" asked a reporter.

"Mr. Stringer, how do you feel about the Freemasons? Are they a threat?" asked another. Bryan went back inside his house and locked the door.

CHAPTER 17

ONE SIMPLE TRUTH

B ryan shut the curtains and locked the back door. He shuffled around, walking back and forth in a panic.

"All we need to do is relax, and the people will get tired of standing outside after a while and then leave. Everything is going to be fine," said Tyler.

"We all know that's not what you're thinking," said Bryan. He walked over to the television and turned it on, then realized that he was on the news.

"There are now burnings of Freemasonry lodges all across the country, and it's all thanks to this kid, twenty-two-year-old Bryan Stringer," said the news reporter.

"There you are! There's your picture!" exclaimed Tyler.

"He and his friends have caused a calamity through this leaked government dossier explaining how he solved a cipher that led to the discovery of Israel's greatest treasure, the ark of the covenant. The ark is no longer in the United States' hands. However, there are reports that it is being transported to the caves of Israel. Up next the president is giving a speech to address a new world religion, and Pope Francis is attending," said the news reporter.

Bryan turned off the television in frustration. "Nobody knows the truth; nobody understands," he said.

"Then make them," replied Tyler.

"How?"

"Well, you said, 'Peace if possible; truth at all costs,' right?"

"Well, yeah. But..."

"But what? It looks like you will just have to tell the truth, then, doesn't it?"

Bryan smiled at Tyler, and at that moment, they understood how much their friendship meant to both of them because they had both fought through their individual trials, but it was like they were in it together.

Later that day the president made his speech addressing his concerns about religion on the White House lawn.

"Today is a historic day! We have all been divided long enough, ladies and gentlemen of the United States and the world. I have behind me the leaders of five religious groups, and we have declared that it is best if we ban together and destroy all that divides us. God has given me a vision of a new world, a new religion, and a new phase for humanity. I announce the new world religion—spirituality."

All the leaders clapped and praised the president heartily; there were harmonious cheers from around the world. "Now is the time to unify together under one government, one world religion, one world order!" declared the president.

* * *

Bryan was back at his house writing his thesis for his religion class, which started at two o'clock. "Have those people left yet?" he asked.

"No, they haven't," said Tyler.

Bryan typed the final words on his computer and then printed out his thesis. "OK, I've gotta go," he said.

"All right, good luck."

"Thanks. I'm gonna need it."

Bryan went to his garage and once again got in his black Ford Escape and looked back as if expecting a yellow folder to be there. He started his car, and his mind flashed back to the mysterious figure who had held a gun to his head just a month or so earlier.

Bryan drove the ten minutes to Georgetown University. He parked his car and hurried into the building with confidence. He walked up onto the oak stage, took a deep breath, and began to read his thesis in front of his peers:

"'Religion is a good thing, right? That's why all of us are studying religion, as well as the history behind it. Religion is a great thing, but in the past month and a half or so, I have realized that we shouldn't be studying religion at all; we should be studying truth.

"Because isn't that what religion is supposed to be—believing in something so strongly that we believe it as truth? You're probably saying to yourself, "Bryan, what are you even talking about?" What is truth? Really, it shouldn't be bound by a definition or the way we feel or the emotions that rise up within us; truth is verified as an indisputable fact.'"

* * *

Back on the White House lawn, the president was finishing up his own speech on religion with the pope and other religious leaders. Then suddenly, from the direction of the crowd of news reporters, a silver bullet penetrated deep into the side of the president's skull. He was immediately covered by Secret Service agents who were assessing the incident, and they quickly called in a medical team and ambulance. The president was rushed as fast as possible to the hospital.

A Secret Service agent looked at camera footage on a laptop of the event in slow motion. "OK, OK, stop right there; that's him," said the agent.

"Wait, isn't that the kid who found the ark of the covenant?" asked the head of the Secret Service.

"I don't know," replied the agent.

"Well, whoever he is, let's find him," said the head of the Secret Service.

* * *

Meanwhile, back at Georgetown University, Bryan was finishing up his own speech on religion:

"'Now think about that for a moment—we can't dispute truth. Why? Because truth in itself is fact. Now you can try to create your own truth, but if you create your own truth, is it really truth, or are you just labeling it that way or justifying it as such? With truth, there has to be a basis from which it comes, so you're probably wondering, "Where does truth come from?" That is the question many people have tried to answer over the years, but only one person has found the answer. Many refuse to believe it, though. Why? Because it's just simply true, and people would rather live and believe in their own truth than face the reality of being wrong.

"'We don't need religion; all we need is truth, and the truth is we all need Jesus. The truth is we have taken the truth and twisted it into something we can no longer control. So I ask you, what do you believe, and why do you believe it, and what is your standard or reason for believing it? Is it real truth or just a facade? Do you believe it because your parents believe it, or is it something you personally believe? Are you living in it, or are you just going through the motions?

"'So I ask you one more time, do you believe in religion? I don't; I believe in a relationship with Jesus, and that's where my hope is found. So I guess my final question to you is, where do you find your hope?'"

Bryan heard applause from the back of the room; it was Dean Andrews. "Well done," he said. Bryan just smiled.

Later, when he was walking to his car, out of nowhere two black Suburbans with flashing lights and loud sirens pulled up and blocked the street. Four Secret Service agents got out of the cars. One of them shouted to Bryan from a distance.

"Bryan Stringer?" asked the Secret Service agent.

"Yes," Bryan replied.

"You're under arrest for the murder of the president of the United States."

A man stood off in the distance holding a silicone mask of Bryan's face. "Protecting the brotherhood," said the man, standing there and smiling as Bryan got arrested. Bryan stood there in the parking lot, astonished, as they cuffed his wrists, but then he realized something—he realized that the world isn't as black-and-white as it may appear. It's full of grayness and color, of complex problems, and like a book, it carries complex narratives and confusing conspiracies, but only he could determine his future though free will and God's purpose; the story God had placed him in was still being written.

The story would never truly be over until the heavenly author said it was. So whether he died for something he had been framed for or not, he would hold his head high and take a deep breath in and simply believe in the one who had created him. He simply accepted his fate, his faults, and the simple truth, love, and sacrifice of Jesus Christ, even if he never even deserved it.

Bryan was slowly walked to one of the black Suburbans, and his head was pushed down by one of the Secret Service agents. The other agents got into their vehicles, and as they were driving down the road, one of the agents turned on the radio. "The president survived. I repeat, the president survived. And as a tribute to his hospital room, number 666, people are marking themselves with the number; you should too."

"I don't think you should; to me, it just sounds like a waste of a marker," said Bryan, chuckling.

And within an instant, within a blink of an eye, Bryan's soul faded away up into the air and met up with many others in the sky; he was not put under God's wrath, because he truly believed. He was raptured, leaving behind his physical clothing and material possessions. From mortality into immortality his soul went.

And so began the beginning of the end as clouds as black as ashes loomed overhead.

ABOUT THE AUTHOR

Quinn Muccio is an American author and screenwriter whose great-great-grandfather was a thirty-three-degree Freemason.

CIRCULATOR

COMMUNITY
BLOOD
CENTER
OF THE OZARKS

A quarterly publication celebrating life through blood donation

Volume 5, Issue 3, Fall 2005

Small body, big heart

Blood donors help Fayetteville toddler beat the odds

Prematurely delivered at twenty-six weeks and two-and-a-half pounds, doctors thought that tiny Quinn Michael Muccio didn't stand much of a chance.

Quinn developed Necrotizing Enterocolitis (NEC) just after birth. NEC is a gastrointestinal disease that causes infection, inflammation and in this case perforation of the intestines. Quinn also developed Fungemia, which is a disease involving the presence of fungi or yeasts in the bloodstream. Finally, there was also severe bleeding on Quinn's brain. "Doctors said that there was no hope," says Quinn's mother Courtney Muccio. "They said that if he lived there would be severe damage, affecting hearing, vision, speech and movement. At eleven days they took his intestines apart to treat the NEC. The picture was pretty bleak."

Newborn Quinn Muccio, born at twenty-six weeks, weighed just two-and-a-half pounds

Early in Quinn's treatment, mom Courtney and father Mike decided that they would let this child fight as long as he wanted to. "We decided that we were going to love Quinn and take care of him no matter what happened," Courtney explains. "We realized that God is bigger than Quinn's problems. So many were praying for him. All through the first three months of his life I just felt an unbelievable strength, and I think he felt it too. We just never thought he wasn't going to make it."

Along with the prayers went treatment. Over one hundred blood and platelet donations helped Quinn keep his strength through the agonizing process. Slowly, the Muccios saw Quinn begin to come around. "At the height of his treatment, he was getting three platelet transfusions a day," Courtney says. "I know that because he had Type O-Negative blood, there were several times that donors had to be specially called to give on his behalf." After two-and-a-half months of treatment at Northwest Medical Center in Springdale and Children's Hospital in St. Louis, Quinn finally was able to go home in January of 2004.

Amazingly, most of the problems doctors outlined in that first bleak prognosis did not come to pass. His hearing and eyesight are both good. He's a little behind kids his age in terms of fine and gross motor skills, but therapy is quickly allowing him to catch up. Quinn just celebrated his second birthday in October.

The Muccios realize that they were fortunate. They also realize the impact that blood from CBCO donors had on Quinn's ability to fight through the ordeal. "Quinn is our little miracle, but he wouldn't have survived unless he had platelets," Courtney says. "That's just the facts. I realize that blood donation takes some time. I definately appreciate the people that are so unselfish. Thank you very much for donating blood."

Now healthy and happy, Quinn is a living testament to the power of blood donation